The Inwood Book

Poems, Short Stories & A Novel

by

John F. McMullen

"johnmac the bard"

Dedications

- To all the friends, acquaintances, parents, store owners, Paulist Priests, Christian Brothers, Sisters of Mercy, sports coaches, bartenders, and all the others who made the Inwood experience special.

- To the members of the Inwood Social Network and the many Inwood Internet Mailing lists who keep the flame burning.

- To the writers, Pete Hamill, Thomas Kelly, Jimmy Breslin, Andrew Greeley, Dennis Hamill, Lawrence Block, and many others, who, without knowing it, influenced me by their ear for neighborhood language and skill in reproducing it.

- To the writers whom I interact with locally and on Facebook, gaining from their ideas and encouragement.

- And, of course, to my family, my wonderful and talented wife, Barbara E. McMullen, and my children, Claire Cleary McMullen and Luke John McMullen.

Books by
John F.McMullen

"Cashing A Check" (2009)

"Writing In My Head" (2009)

"With A Chip On My Shoulder" (2009)

"New and Collected Poems" (2010)

"The Inwood Book" (2010)

Inwood, Manhattan, New York City

The Inwood of which I write is not the Inwood of today. Today's Inwood – the northern tip of Manhattan Island, New York City – is an amalgam of Yuppies, Dominicans, and the older Irish and Jewish. The Inwood of the 1940's, '50s, and '60s—my Inwood – was Irish Catholic / Jewish with a decidedly Irish Catholic culture (or so it seemed; the Jewish culture was under my radar). This culture was centered in two major institutions: Good Shepherd Roman Catholic Church and the bars, of which there were legion.

It was a simpler time –pre-pill, pre-drugs. We went to school, played sports, attended church, thought about sex, and drank beer. The only language spoken in the neighborhood was English, often with a brogue; in parts of today's Inwood, much of the population speaks Spanish.

As I write this in December 2009, I'm sitting in a Barnes and Noble, sipping a vente latte (4 shots) and typing on a netbook computer. Fifty years ago, I would have been on my way home from Iona College, looking forward to a date with the young lady I was going out with, followed by an evening sitting on a stool in the Broadstone, drinking beer and trading stories and opinions with friends, old and new.

Admittedly, similar scenarios were being played out in other areas of New York City – in Pete Hamill's Brooklyn, in Fordham, on the West Side `of Manhattan, and in Jimmy Breslin's Queens. Yet to us, the Inwood Diaspora, our neighborhood and our experiences still seem unique and, whenever we can, we get together – monthly luncheons, on-line social networks and mailing lists, and annual reunions – to relive the experiences of our youth.

The poems, short stories, essays, and novel contained within reflect the times of my formative (and often misspent) youth.

Background -- Inwood

Inwood, the northern-most neighborhood on the island of Manhattan, is, for those of us who grew up in the 1950s and '60s, as much a state of mind as a physical location. It was an Irish Catholic / Jewish neighborhood with very little interaction between the cultures. The neighborhood is distinguished by Inwood Park, a very large park containing the only forest on Manhattan Island. The park also, by legend, is the place where Peter Minuet purchased Manhattan Island from the Indians.

In my years growing up in Inwood, it was a neighborhood of schools, bars, churches, bars, ice cream parlors, bars, and candy stores – did I say bars? Inwood had more bars than any neighborhood in New York City and was so well known that the famous Walter Winchell supposedly referred to it as "GINwood". In the pre-pill age of Irish Catholic no-sex Puritanism, beer and sports took the place of sexual exploration.

Inwood is bounded on three sides by rivers, the Harlem on the east and north and the Hudson on the west, and the neighborhood of Washington Heights on the south. It is home to three Roman Catholic parishes – *Good Shepherd, the only Roman Catholic Church on Broadway in New*

York City, St. Jude's, home of the legendary St. Jude's Bazaar, and Our Lady Queen of Martyrs on the south – Columbia University's Baker Field Athletic Complex (*at the northern tip of the island*), the aforementioned Inwood Park as well as portions of Fort Tryon Park (*containing the Cloisters*), the historic Dyckman House, and many bars.

Inwood has been the scene of a number of marvelous books, such as **Thomas Kelly**'s "*Rackets,*" **Pete Hamill**'s "*Forever*" and **William Dyer**'s "*The Kingdom of Inwood.*" "**Inwood – Past and Present**," an on-line Social Network located at ***inwood10034.ning.com*** contains many pictures and tales of the "old neighborhood." People from Inwood have a strong attachment to the neighborhood as manifested by the social network, Internet lists, periodic reunions, and monthly luncheons. It is the neighborhood in which I grew up and in which my novel "***Offering It Up***" is set.

Background II -- "The Drink"

Much has been written in other places about the drinking that went on in Inwood and in other Irish Catholic neighborhoods in general. The wonderful *"Drinking Life"* by **Pete Hamill** details his experiences growing up in a bar-centered Irish Catholic Brooklyn neighborhood and others have similar stories (although none, in my judgment, told as well as Hamill's).

There are a number of points to be remembered when considering the prodigious drinking that went on in Inwood in those times:

- The legal drinking age in New York State at the time was eighteen, giving us a head start on other states.
- The legal age of eighteen meant that we could start drinking illegally at ages reaching down as far as fourteen.
- The social center in Ireland, particularly throughout the years of hardship, was "The Pub." This tradition carried over to the bars and saloons of New York City and Inwood was said the have more bars than any other neighborhood in New York.

- The vast Inwood Park, with acres of forest (called "the woods") provided the underage ideal places to consume the illegal beer.
- In the pre-pill days, there was very, very, very little pre-marital sex in the neighborhood. The threat of pregnancy coupled with the constant admonition of the nuns that "you will go straight to hell" kept the blouses buttoned and the boys playing sports and drinking.
- The absence of sex played another part as couples, unprepared for marriage, married anyhow mainly to "get laid." They continued to live in the neighborhood and the new husbands continued to hang out in the same bars as before the nuptials.
- Many of the young male workers in Inwood were either civil servants – police, fire, or transit workers – or construction workers; all jobs that, for one reason or another, tend to be "high drinking jobs."

What many, including wives and girlfriends, did not understand was that, for most of us, the alcohol was actually incidental to the spirit of camaraderie that it built – the beer gave us a reason to be in the bar or in the park with our friends and, the more beer that we drank, the longer the night lasted. Additionally, after a week of being held in check in strict Catholic High Schools and Colleges, it gave us a way to lower our inhibitions and, on occasion, do really stupid things.

On summer nights, there would be groups of twenty or so in various locations – "in the circle," "behind the handball courts," "on the steps" or "halfway up the path" (my venue of choice), talking and drinking until the beer ran out – 18 cans of Pabst was my normal ration (when I complimented my main supplier, deli-owner Lennie Jones, on his store's new picture window, he told me that I "had paid for it with my purchases of Pabst." I thought that it was a positive … then). When it got colder, it was off to the bars until closing time (4AM most nights; 3AM on pre-Mass Saturday night) and then the heartiest of us would get "six to go" and head for "the circle" to continue the discussions and watch the sun come up.

Each of the bars had its own identity and folks would hang out in a particular bar for long periods of time until, for one reason or another, the group would move to another. During my drinking years in Inwood (ages 16 -24), I hung around for stretches of time in Erin's Isle, The Willow Tree, Bowlarama, The Broadstone, Grippo's, Cassidy's, and Chamber's. We might stop into other bars such as Minogue's or Doc Fiddler's for a quick drink or to see a friend but we normally stayed true to whatever campus we had adopted for the present. Of all the bars which absorbed significant portions of my income, my favorite was the Broadstone, situated on West 207th Street between Sherman and Post Avenues. Owned by Mrs. Cahill, a widow and the mother of a contemporary, it was usually manned by one of my favorite bartenders, Pat Gallagher, a kind and quiet man with a good sense of humor.

To be sure, a number of my friends and acquaintances "fell into the bottle" and either eventually went into a "twelve-step program" or died of it.

But, it was great fun while it lasted!.

Background III -- Good Shepherd

Good Shepherd Roman Catholic Church, a very large gray stone edifice on Broadway (the only Catholic Church on Broadway in New York City) on the corner of Islam Street in Inwood and the school sitting behind it across Cooper Street were, during all my years in the neighborhood, the cultural and sports center of Inwood.

Speaking in the church after a candlelight parade commemorating the horror that was "9/11," New York State Assemblyman Stanley Michaels, a member of the Jewish persuasion, said, "No matter what religion you were, Good Shepherd has always been the center of the neighborhood." To be sure, there were not only other Catholic parishes in Inwood (St. Jude's on the eastern side and Our Lady Queen of Martyrs ("OLQM") on the southern side but also Episcopalian and Lutheran churches and a Jewish Temple. Yet Good Shepherd was, as Michaels said, the real center of the neighborhood.

I and the large majority of my friends were baptized in Good Shepherd, received First Communion and Confirmation in the Church, celebrated marriages there, and buried our parents from there. We went to Good Shepherd Grammar School and, male and female, played basketball, baseball, and softball for CYO (Catholic Youth Organization) teams representing Good Shepherd; its Sunday afternoon basketball league was open to boys of all religions. Two of my Protestant friends and one Jewish one played in the league and we all went to the "Friday Night Dances" (in fact, people came from all over the larger area – Washington Heights, Fordham, Marble Hill, Kingsbridge, and Riverdale to come to the dances. The same "outlanders" would in later years also frequent the famed co-ed watering holes in the neighborhood – Chambers, Doc Fiddler's, The Inwood Lounge, and Gary Owen's).

The Christian Brothers, the Sisters of Mercy, and some dedicated "lay teachers" were our instructors in the grammar school and the Paulist Fathers, an order known for its intellectual prowess, staffed the church (sadly, none of these groups are still associated with the parish). I and many of my friends were altar boys while others sang in the choir. The boys all went to Junior Holy Name Breakfasts and the girls to those run by the Legion of Mary. Those with dramatic inclinations joined the Paulist Players.

It was a different time. The children and their parents all attended Mass every Sunday and we stayed "dressed up" (suits and ties) for most of the day – even our Jewish and Protestant friends dressed for Sunday. We only climbed out of the Sunday "digs" to play ball – baseball, when young with Mr. McLoughlin, a very special father, and when older as CYO team members, basketball at the always packed courts, or football, whether touch or tackle in the Hudson Valley League. Finally, another part of Sundays was the mandatory family sit-down dinner – "Now, you be back at three o'clock. I don't want to have to send your father looking for you." – and then, on Monday morning, it was back to Good Shepherd, boys in white shirts and ties and blue pants and girls in uniform skirts and blouses.

Different times!

The Poems

by

John F. McMullen
"johnmac the bard"

Contents

Inwood Park

The top of Manhattan Island
-- not, though, the top of
the borough of Manhattan
(but that's another story)
where the Indians fleeced
Peter Minuit.

Fields for baseball, football,
and Irish sports.
Courts for basketball, tennis,
handball, and horseshoes
(we called those "pits").

And, the "woods" – a forest with
paths, caves, and hidden places --
where we learned to smoke
(implanting cancer cells into
many of our lungs) and
drink (beginning the deterioration of
brain and liver cells for many).

And couples often moved from the
benches in the park to the woods
for more privacy ... but, in those days,
there was no fucking (or, at least,
none that I knew about).

We would have been better
off fucking (if we had known
about safe sex) – some of us
who weren't fucking later
died of lung cancer or cirrhosis.

It's still a wonderful park.

My Corner

My corner in the
1940s, and 50s, and 60s was
215th Street and Seaman Avenue
Inwood
Manhattan
New York City.

All we had to say growing up
was "meetcha on the corner"
we never had to say which corner.
Other places were
"down the park"
"on the wall"
"up in the circle"
"in the playground"
"at the courts"
but this was "on the corner."

Seaman Ave. and 215th St.
lined with 5 and 6 story
apartment houses, each
peopled by gaggles of kids.

Our group in the early years was small
before Mike and Warren
before even Rick and Hobart
there was Fran (later Frank),
Tod (never Tom), Billy, and Bob,
2 Jims (one "Jamesy" for "James E.),
2 Johns (one "The Moose"),
a Kevin (who let his parents
kipnap him to Larchmont),
a Eugene (later Gene), and a Dan.

One Italian last name, one German
the rest Irish and all Catholic
-- not exactly multi-cultural!

Sons of cops, fireman, clerks,
transit workers, bartenders,
cab drivers ... and one lawyer.
Terrorized by "the big kids,"
we often took revenge on
"the little kids."

We went to school together,
played sports together and, later
(except for the Larchmont expatriate),
drank a lot of beer together.

Some had strict parents;
some did not.
Some were the first born;
others were the middle
or the babies.

Yet we all graduated from college
and many have advanced degrees,
We turned into doctors, lawyers,
college professors, journalists,
engineers, accountants, businessmen,
and social workers.

What was unique that made us all
pursue education – not all of our
siblings or friends did
and they had the same
nuns in school and same parents.
Who knows?

Some of us have lived all over the country,
even all over the world, while some have
never left New York State.
Now we are scattered on the East Coast
New York, New Jersey, New Hampshire,
Virginia, and North Carolina.
Two have even "gone home."

Yet, after 60 years I still know that
if I ever need anything,
all I have to do
is pick up the phone and call
one of the guys that
I'd meet on the corner.

The Bars

I grew up in an Irish/Jewish neighborhood.
The Jewish lads went to school and studied;
the Irish went to the bars.

To be sure, many of us also went to school
and played sports and went out with girls
(no sex, though).
But we went to the bars
underage
after games
after dates
after softball games
before and after dances
to watch the Sunday football game
and for every other damn reason.

The Broadstone
the Willow Tree, Erin's Isle
Chambers', McSherry's, the Inwood Lounge
Doc Fiddler's, Cassidy's, Jimmy Ryan's, Keenan's Corner
Dolan's, The Pig n' Whistle, Freehill's, Terminal, Old
Shilling
Markey's, McGolderick's, Carmor, Rooney's, Grippo's,
Minogue's.
Well, you get the idea.

We knew the bartenders by name.
George Lynch, Pat Gallagher, "Sunshine," Georgie Costello,
Chris, Fred, Tommy, Mara, Dan, John, Joe, Kathy-in-Erin's
and they all bought back. "The next one's on me, Mac"
(and you never leave after a buyback).

We hung out there
we talked
we laughed
we sang
we sometimes fought
... and we drank.

But we didn't just drink in the bars
we drank in the park
we drank at parties
we drank at football games
we drank at dances (from a hidden flask).

Many slowed down as they grew up
many stopped altogether
and some were stopped only by the grave.

"The drink" was a macho factor.
If you told a fellow he had diabetes,
he'd stop taking sugar.
If you told some of my friends that
they shouldn't drink, they'd say
"What do you mean? I can hold my liquor."

They planned to drink until they died
and they did.

I still think we had more fun
than the Jewish guys
(unless they were getting laid).

The Friday Night Dance

On Friday night, we'd get
suited up and head down to
our local Catholic Grammar School
for a teenage dance
(when we got a bit older,
we'd kill a ½ pint of
Old Mr. Boston Lemon
Flavored Vodka first).

I'd be wrapped around a girl
in a slow dance, my hand caressing
her hair as my torso tried to join hers
when Father Devine would wander
over and say,
"Leave room for the Holy Ghost."

That statement might have opened up
space between some other bodies
but I would make the point that
"the Holy Ghost is spiritual, Father;
he can fit anywhere he wants"
(fifty years later, after winning a Silver
Star as a Vietnam chaplain, he still
remembers those remarks).

If a young lady returns after such a dance
to dance again, she had to really like me
for I would have been singing in her ear
with the worst singing voice in the world.

Oh, well; it was prior to the pill and
these girls didn't put out anyhow.
… so we drank.

The Little Black Boy

When I was just 11,
a little white boy,
a little black boy
changed my life.

I grew up in an Irish /
Jewish neighborhood --
that is understating it.
There were few Italians,
less Jews, and almost no
Protestants and NO Blacks.

I heard about Blacks -- I
cheered for Jackie Robinson
and didn't see what the big
deal was -- Why didn't they
always let them play?

But I also heard the terms
that we now know as racist --
"coon," "boogie," and, of
course, "the N word."

But I didn't see any of this
as a big deal either -- we
called each other "shanty,"
"lace curtain," "stupid micks,"
etc.

Then I went to a Catholic
grammar school track meet
outside my neighborhood
-- at night.
I had to fight to get my
parents to let me go.

So, I'm standing in a line
-- a long line -- for a soda
and this little black kid,
about eight years old
was being a real pain
in the ass
jumping all around
making noise
behaving like, well,
an 8 year-old.

Finally, he stepped on my toes.
I grabbed him by his shoulders,
shook him, and pushed him,
saying
"Get out of here, you little
nigger."

He ran off, crying.
I was still in line
when he came back
with his big brother.

I immediately knew
that it was all over
-- these guys carry knives.
I was dead.

He came up to me and
said,
"Did you call my brother
a nigger?"
I gulped and said
"Yes."

He looked at me harshly
and said,
"You're a Catholic;
you should know better"
... and walked away.

And, from then on,
I knew better.

(If he has just
"kicked the shit out of me,"
as I expected, all I would
have learned was to
"look for the big brother first.")

1958

I drive deep into the right corner go up in the air, hang for an
instant, and get nothing but net!
Afterwards, one of the players on our younger team,
Vinnie Bernadetto asks me how I stay up in the air so long.
Vinnie died last week.

I clear a rebound, turn, and hit Buddy Kelly streaking
downcourt for a layup.
Buddy died over 10 years ago.

Bob Cummings takes a rebound, gives to me and
I find John Marai with a bounce pass as he cuts
to the basket – two more points!
Both Bob and John are dead for over ten years.

After the game, coach Jim McArdle pats me on the
ass and says, "Nice game."
Jim's been dead for over twenty years.

Bob Gorman and Jerry Moran walk up the stairs with me to
the locker room.
They're both gone too.

Sometimes I remember too much.

Remembrance of Fallen Heroes

On Saturday, I went to the annual
"Remembrance of Fallen Heroes"
gathering held in Inwood Park,
a tribute to the twenty-three
"First Responders" from Inwood
who died on 9/11.

While there was sadness in the
memory of the uncalled for deaths,
there was joy in the camaraderie
of the assemblage.

It is what we do best –
caring for those we know well
-- for those we hardly know
-- and for those we didn't know at all,
all tied together by our Inwood heritage.

Yet, we hear platitudes at times like this,
as well as at Michael Jackson's and
Jim Carroll's funeral – about how
these people "will be remembered forever."

They won't be!
Most of us have no clue what
our great grandparents did while alive.
We rarely dwell on the sacrifices that
the dead of the Civil War, Great Wars,
or Korea made for us. The heroes of
9/11 will share the same fate.

No – they won't be remembered forever
so it is very good that we remember them now!

Tales of "The Stone"

Short Stories

The stories contained within this section are either totally true, true with the names changed to protect the guilty, or totally made up. In each case, they reflect the spirit of the neighborhood and bars and as I knew them.

by
John F. McMullen
"johnmac the bard"

Contents

Chickie Goes To War

John Charles "Chickie" (aka "Chick") Donohue was (and is) one of the great characters to come out of Inwood. Over the years that I have known him, he has been a "parkie" (the local name for employees of New York City's Department of Parks), a Marine, a merchant seaman, a bar owner, a hot dog stand vendor, a Sandhog, a holder of a Harvard MPA, an official of the Teamsters Union, and a producer of a television series about the Sandhogs. Additionally, he has been a character in a Thomas Kelly novel and has had a novel by Jimmy Breslin dedicated to him. The Harvard MPA is particularly unusual as Chickie was academically dismissed from Rice High School (amazingly glib, he was not at that time a reader), obtained a GED while a merchant seaman and never attended college.

There are hundreds of Chickie stories and I witnessed or was a party to many of them – taking him to the hospital when a bartender broke his nose; accompanying him to a Catholic parish dance that led to the biggest brawl that I was ever in; sleeping in his bungalow in Rockaway; and closing many bars with him.

When Chickie returned from the Marine Corp's "bootcamp," my crowd spent many nights in the Broadstone listening to Chick's tales of Paris Island and his enjoyment of the Marines. During this time, he became a particular friend of the bartender, Pat Gallagher, and, when he was about to ship out to Okinawa, Chick took off his dog tags and gave them to Pat to hang on the large gold clock chain behind the bar, saying he would reclaim them when he returned.

Over the next eighteen months, one of us often pointed out the dog tags to a newcomer and explained the story to him so, by the time that Chick returned, the dog tag retrieval had turned into a mini-festival. On that day, a gaggle of us paraded to the bar and Pat bought a round for all as Chick ceremonially returned the dog tags to his neck.

The rest of the night, until I left, was full of good cheer, stories of Okinawa, and singing. I'm glad that I left before Chickie got into a fight by the bowling game he was playing, hit the other contestant over the head with the bowling puck, and got barred from the joint.

A few years later, Chick, now a merchant seaman, informed us that he would be shipping out of the West Coast and would be stopping in Saigon. As this was during the Vietnam War, we expressed concern for his safety but he didn't seem concerned, so we simply reminded him that there were a lot of neighborhood folk in the service over there and told him to "buy them a beer for us." While we promptly forgot about the suggestion, Chickie, unbeknownst to us, compiled a list of the locals serving in 'Nam" and, when he got to Saigon, tried to locate them.

Able to locate one local serving in a combat zone, Chickie used his Marine credentials to hitch a ride on a helicopter to the fellow's unit and swung down into the fellow's foxhole with a six-pack. "Want a beer, Mickey?" (*If I were Mickey, I would have thought that I had died and gone to heaven.*)

The foxhole escapade eventually made it into columns by the New York Daily News' Mike

McAlary and Newsday's Dennis Duggan – and the legend of Chickie Donoghue moved beyond Inwood.

For more on Chickie and the Sandhogs, see:

http://www.history.com/content/sandhogs/meet-the-sandhogs/chickie-donohue

Maureen

I was sitting at the end of the bar in the Broadstone, by the juke box, drinking Pabst and listening to Don Gibson's "I Can't Stop Loving You." It was a Thursday evening about 7:30 and I could have been home reading or watching television but the bar held more of an attraction.

Peggy had recently given back my high school ring and it was easier being in the 'Stone' with people than home during the time I was usually on the phone with her. My friends thought that I was devastated by the breakup and had retreated to the bar for alcohol consolation but they misread me. I hadn't been "in love" with Peggy – as a matter of fact, I had never been in love with anyone; at 19, that was still in front of me. My routine, however, had been disrupted. I would normally have read for a while, talked to Peggy on the phone, and then taken a walk to pick up the early additions of the Daily News and Mirror. Some nights, I'd talk on the corner for a while with friends and then call it a night; on others, I'd head to the Broadstone and read the papers at the bar.

Pat Gallagher had just put another one down in front of me, rapped his knuckles on the bar and said "This one's on me, Mac" when the door opened and a drop-dead beautiful red-head stepped into the bar. She slipped onto the empty stool next to me and told Pat, "A bourbon Manhattan, please. Do you have Wild Turkey?" After Pat assured her that he did and went off to mix the drink, she turned to me and asked "Are the restrooms in the back?" I nodded yes and she was off the stool and on her way.

I watched her as she walked. She didn't walk through the bar crowd. She rather walked around the divider to the table area before moving toward the restrooms. Still, she had to notice that virtually every male at the bar had turned to watch her walk. It really was more of a saunter than a walk and she obviously knew that she had a lovely ass and used it to generate our attention.

Pat smiled as he laid her Manhattan down and said in a low voice, "Be careful, Mac." Before I could ask him to explain, she was back and on the seat next to me, closer this time. She sipped at the Manhattan and, looking me in the eye, said "Perfect." She then licked at the cherry and sucked it into her mouth. Seeing the look on my face, she reached out and squeezed my leg, "See something you like?"

Before I could answer, Bill Curley, a very large ironworker, appeared at her left side and, ignoring me, looked into her face. "Hi, I haven't seen you in here before. Are you new in the neighborhood?"

While she turned slightly to face him, her right hand stayed on my leg and actually was moving up toward my hardening cock. "Yes, I just moved in around the corner on Sherman Avenue." He held out his hand. "Welcome to the neighborhood. I'm Bill Curley." The hand came off my leg to shake his "Maureen Collins. Glad to meet you." He didn't release her hand.

As I was trying to deal with my confusion and annoyance, Pat appeared with another Pabst, "Have another, Mac. On me." As my attention moved to Pat, I considered the situation. Maureen was at least 24 or 25, 5 years older than me; Bill was almost 30, 40 pounds heavier than me, and construction tough. I was obviously out of my league. Still, she had been reaching for my cock.

Pat held my attention, asking me about my tests at school and what I was going to do for the summer, until Bill leaned over and whispered "Sorry, kid" and walked out with Maureen.

My disappointment must have been obvious because Pat said "You're better off, Mac."

"Why am I better off?"

"Because she's a man."

"What? A Man?"

"Yes, Did you notice her wrists? They were bigger than yours. The rest of her was made over well but you can always tell by the wrists."

My whole mood changed as I grinned thinking of Curley's reaction if he got into her pants. "Thanks, Pat."

The next time I saw Curley, he just scowled at me as though he was daring me to say a word. When I didn't, he just sent a beer down the bar to me and Pat grinned as he faced me and said "This one's on Bill."

Hit By A Train

It was about nine o'clock on a Saturday morning when I walked into Broger's and saw an almost green Tom Collins looking like the world had ended. I had been at a Pace College "Beer Racket" the night before and had drunk so much beer that I was not only drunk but caused a bit of a scandal when I attempted to take a swing at a person whom I thought was simply a pompous Pacite trying to eject me; it turned out he was the Dean of said college and I was ejected along with those who came to my aid.

Actually, we didn't belong at the Racket as none of us attended Pace – but we had heard that there would be "all you could drink" for five dollars as well as dancing and about twenty-five of us, including the aforementioned Collins, were in attendance.

Anyway, I woke up hangover-sick after about three hours sleep, had a Alka-Seltzer and a shower and got out of the house. I headed for the local ice cream parlor hangout hoping to find some other miscreants to commiserate with.

As soon as I saw Collins, I knew I had found someone in even worse shape than me. He looked like hell and, seeing me, he said simply "Jimmy Sexton got hit by a train."

"What?"

"I got home about seven o'clock this morning. I woke up on a bench on the 190th street IND station on the downtown side. I have no idea how I got there. So I went upstairs crossed over to the uptown side and came home."

"And?"

"I had just walked in when Jimmy's sister, Judy, called and said that Jimmy had gotten hit by a train at the 190th street station and that I was the last one with him."

"My God! Is he dead?"

"No. She said that the train went over him and that he's in Fordham hospital. He seems to be alright."

"How the hell can he be alright if a train went over him?"

"I have no idea. I must have slept through the whole thing."

"What were you doing at that station?"

"We were both drunk. We must have fallen asleep and stayed on the train at 207th Street when it turned around. I guess that one of us woke up and we got off at 190th street. I was asleep on the bench. When I woke up, I was the only one there. I'm not even sure I remembered he was with me. I just went home. What a fucking mess!"

I ordered a seltzer and dry toast while I listened to Tom moan – he was right; it was a fucking mess.

Jack Walsh wandered in, also with a hangover. We decided to go across to the Broadstone for some "Hair of the Dog" and, on the way out, told Freddy, the owner, to send any other obviously wasted souls over to join us.

By early afternoon, many of the night before's revelers had joined us and, even though we were all drinking beer, the thought of Jimmy and the train was keeping us sober. Finally I got up the nerve to the call the Sexton house for information.

I spoke to Neil, the older brother who was both forthcoming and angry at all of us for not keeping his brother from winding up under a train. It seemed that Jimmy had awakened on the tracks to see the train bearing down on him. He rolled to the middle and flattened out and three cars passed over him without scratching him. He was not in Fordham hospital for injuries but for observation – was he nuts? Suicidal? What the hell was he doing on the tracks?

Neil said that he was on the first floor ward and could have visitors beginning tomorrow.

Relived at the news, we decided to meet in Broger's the next day after the last Mass and descend *en masse* on the hospital and we, more or less, fell back into the normal winter Saturday routine of watching a football game at the bar.

The next day, about two o'clock, Ed Winne, Jack Walsh, Tom Collins, a few others and I bordered the number 19 bus and were off to Fordham Hospital, all a tad apprehensive of what we would find.

What we found was representative of an Andersonville prison – a huge ward with beds everywhere that we could just wander through looking for Jimmy. People were moaning – one person was screaming; his leg was gangrenous -- people were smoking in bed -- there was loud talking -- radios playing – a scary place.

When we located Jimmy, he was in fine shape and sitting up. He had just lit a cigarette for the patient next to him, a motorcycle rider who had broken both arms in an accident. Jimmy was putting the cigarette in and out of the rider's mouth. I thought that Collins, an immense and very tough lad, was going to cry when he saw how good Jimmy looked.

Jimmy laughed when he heard how Tom had found out about the incident.

Three years later, another of our friends, Mike Riordan, wound up on the same tracks. This time, a motorman saw him and stopped the train. When awakened, Mike asked if the motorman "knew what time it was."

Years later, Mike was a successful Wall Street information technology manager and Jimmy had been a partner in a law firm and a respected Wall Street legal tax expert. Hell, they beat the "A" Train; the rest was easy!

Offering It Up

An Inwood Tale

by

John F. McMullen
"johnmac the bard"

Offering It Up

Contents

Offering It Up

Chapter 1 -- I Fall Down

It was early June in 1986, less than a year after I had watched my mother join my father in the family plot at Gate of Heaven Cemetery just down the hill from my Uncle Jack and Aunt Claire, and I was jogging around the baseball field in Inwood Park as part of a promise to myself to regain some physical well-being when I saw, about 50 yards in front on me, a man on the ground with a Hispanic teenager apparently rifling his pockets. Without thinking I yelled "Hey" and, when the teenager looked up, turned, and ran, I yelled at a couple walking by to "call for help" and I took off after him.

He ran across the baseball field toward the Woods with me in-less-than-hot-pursuit. It was obvious that this forty-five year old man was not going to catch the teenager, now running like a rabbit, but I kept after him, hoping for a miracle. I saw him go down the hill on the other side of the field and start for the Woods. I crossed the path and, as I started down the hill, common sense dawned and I gave up the chase -- or planned to when my bad ankle gave out and I fell. I rolled over twice and lay there, in pain and feeling like a jerk for winding up like this.

I have weak ankles from years of basketball poundings. They roll on me if I misstep and down I go. I tape them and wear braces when I play but didn't bother when I went off to jog around a paved road -- my first mistake of what might be many of the day; the second was obviously chasing this Hispanic rabbit.

When I sprain my ankle, I generally have severe eye-closing cursing pain for about a minute and a half and then it subsides. I was just coming out of it when I heard "Mister ... mister ... are you ok?" I looked up and here was the kid I was chasing.

He was a well-built athletic looking kid -- probably 16 or 17 with dark brown hair and eyes. He had on gray sweats and looked concerned as he looked at me.

"I sprained my ankle. Help me up." and I held out my hand and let him pull me up. Standing, I was five inches taller than him; I'm about 6'3".

I didn't let go of his arm. He suddenly looked panicked as he felt my grip. "I didn't do anything to that guy ... honest."

"Then, why did you run?"

"As soon as I saw you, I knew how it looked -- a spic kid going through a dead guy's pockets."

"Dead guy? He's dead?"

"He looked like he was. I talked to him and he didn't answer. I felt his head and shook him -- nothing. And then I started looking for ID ... and then I saw you and ran. I guess I panicked."

I believed him.

"Well, then the cops will show up and will want to talk to you. We have to go back over there."

His eyes widened. "I didn't see anything. I just saw the guy lying there. They won't believe that ... and I have a Regents."

"A Regents?"

"Yeah. A History Regents at one o'clock. I was up late studying and came out for a run to wake up. I gotta go home and shower and get to school." He looked at me "Please."

"Where do you go to school?"

"All Hallows -- in the Bronx."

My high school; I could test him. "Who's the Moose?"

"You know Brother Sullivan?"

"Yes. Now who are you and where do you live?"

"Frankie Almonte. I live at 117 Seaman."

I heard sirens from across the park and said "Ok, Frankie, get out of here. Go right home and get to school." I released his arm.

"You're letting me go?"

"Yes -- for now. But you'd better hurry or you may not be able to leave."

"Oh, yeah. Thanks." and he turned and ran off.

Chapter 2 -- The Priest At The Scene

I climbed back up the hill with some difficulty and in some pain. Coming over the ridge, I saw a crowd where the man had been lying and two 34th Precinct prowl cars. I started limping across the field and saw the woman of the couple that I had called to pointing at me as she spoke to a uniformed cop.

As I limped across the field, I saw that the man was still on the ground with a group of people gathered around him. One of the people wore a Roman collar, my brother Matty Devine, CSP, the white sheep of the family. Matty had arranged a transfer to the local parish, Good Shepherd, from Washington when my mother first became sick.

The uniformed cop stopped me as I arrived on the scene. "Sir, you were seen running away from here a few minutes ago. Why was that? And can I see some identification please?"

Repressing my initial reaction of "Fuck you too," I said "I don't have any identification in my sweatpants but the priest over there can probably identify me. He's my confessor."

"The priest looks busy, sir. And you haven't explained why you ran away."

"I didn't run away. I was chasing somebody who I thought might have been mugging the guy on the ground."

"Where is this alleged mugger, sir?"

My annoyance, partially brought on by the throb in my ankle and partially at the need to continually suppress "asshole" in my responses to the cop, had to be beginning to show.

"He got away when I fell down the goddamn hill."

"Please describe him, sir."

Without hesitation, I lied. "He was about my size, blond hair, and he ran like a deer." Well, he did run like a deer.

I started to move away from the cop toward the body.

"I'm sorry, sir, we're not finished and we'll have to keep you here for your formal statement."

I kept limping away. "Why don't you have Jimmy Finn call me? Jack Devine -- he has the number."

"You know Sgt. Finn?"

"Yes, I used to kick his ass on the basketball courts over there."

I finally reached my brother, standing with two other cops over what was obviously a dead man. "Oh, shit. That's Frank Ford."

Matty looked up. "Jackie. Did you say something?"

I nodded no. Things were going too fast. Frank had been in my class at All Hallows -- another All Hallows connection. He had been a bully then but his bluster was worse than his bite. I had only seen him a few times over the years. We were never really friends but he had called me just a few months ago and now he was dead.

"You look like hell, Jackie. What happened? "

"I fell down a goddamned hill, Father ... and sprained my fucking ankle." The two cops looked at me as though I had insulted the Pope.

Matty grinned. "He's my brother, fellows. Jackie Devine." We shook hands.

"Are you almost finished, Matty? Come up for coffee? I want to get off this ankle."

"About 5 or 10 -- go on up. I'll be along in a bit."

So, with the approval of the Holy Father, the cops allowed me to hobble off.

Offering It Up

Chapter 3 -- I Go To Confession

I entered 583 West 215th Street and, stopping at the mailbox, ran into Mrs. Taylor. She, Mrs. Cummings, and Mrs. Roach were the last of the people in the building from my youth and had been friends of my mother. Because of the affection for her and for my sainted older brother, they had often overlooked my many teenage (and older) indiscretions.

"Good morning, Mrs. Taylor. How are you, today?"

"Oh, hello Jackie. Fine and how's Matty? I saw him last Sunday at the 12:45 and he looked tired."

"He's fine. I just left him. He's in the park, administering last rites to a person in the park."

"Someone died in the park?"

I related the story, assuring her that it was no one that she knew and leaving out my chase and fall. By then, I had collected my mail and I said goodbye.

"Be careful, Jackie." People had been telling me that all my life.

"Thanks, Mrs. Taylor. I will."

As I rode up in the elevator, I went through the mail and found a padded brown envelope with my name and address handwritten on it. The envelope contained a 3 1/2" diskette and a note that said simply, "I'm in trouble, Jackie, and I can't think of anyone else who can help me." It was signed "Frank Ford."

"Oh, shit" was my first reaction. "What do I do now?"

I walked down the hall to my apartment and unlocked the door. I have the nicest apartment in Inwood, a 4 bedroom with a great entry hall on the top floor on the corner of 215th and Indian Road.

My parents moved up from a 2 bedroom on the third floor when the Lamberts moved to Massachusetts about 20 years ago. The move gave my brother and younger sister, Margaret Mary (now Peggy) each our own rooms. I moved back in after my father died and my mother had gotten sick. This was about three years ago and I stayed.

After my mother died, some of the neighbors had proposed trading apartments with me since I "couldn't possibly need all that space." I had politely refused -- not politely enough, it seems as some still don't talk to me, explaining that my children would be spending time with me and required their own rooms. I also needed a place for my computers and books -- I work out of my house as a computer consultant -- but I never got to explain that.

I also had to negotiate with the landlord who would have received a rental increase from a new tenant. While my name was not on the existing lease, I had been paying the rent by check for three years and had been living full time there so I think that he knew that he would be on shaky ground should be try to evict me. That, coupled with the fact that such action would alienate many of the older residents, led him to accept a reasonable increase from me to put the lease in my name.

I opened the door, put down the mail and dialed CY(prus) 3-4545, All Hallows. "Is Brother Sullivan available?"

I was connected through to the Moose who was at lunch in the Brother's dining room.

"Brother Sullivan."

"Brother, It's Jack Devine. How are you?"

"Jackie. I'm fine. How's Matty? And how are you doing?"

"I'm well and Matty is too. I ran across one of your students this morning in a rather strange situation and I was wondering what you could tell me about him. Frankie Almonte."

"Franklin? What a good kid! He comes from a fairly poor family and lived in Spanish Harlem. He went to St. Cecilia's when Brother Walsh was the principal. Brother Walsh kept banging on our door for a scholarship for the kid and we gave him one. It turned out to be a great deal for both him and the school."

"He's on the honor roll and on the track team." Damn -- that figures. "He works in a deli on 161st Street over here and his father got a better job as a super someplace in Inwood and they moved out of Spanish Harlem. I'd love for us to hang onto him and ship him to Iona but he may wind up with a free ride to NYU or one of the Ivies. His being Dominican with the grades and the track makes him attractive now."

So I was right about the kid. The doorbell rang and I leaned over to let Matty in as I kept talking.

"So how'd you meet Franklin and why the interest?"

"I just ran into him in the park this morning and we got talking. Ahh, Matty just walked in. Say hello."

I handed Matty the phone. "It's the Moose." I didn't want to lie to Brother Sullivan but I didn't want to share the details of this morning's meeting with him. I wasn't sure if I wanted to share it with anyone.

I put coffee on and, when Matty had finished with the Moose, sat down with him at the kitchen table for a breather.

"Do you get used to those calls, Matty? Rushing out to administer last rites?"

"Not really. I usually don't know the person. It's easier for me to relate if I had been visiting the person while sick but the out-of-the-blue ones, when I don't know the person, are tough. I try to care as much but it's hard."

"You knew this guy, Matty -- or maybe you didn't. He was in my class, two years behind you at All Hallows. He is, or was, Frankie Ford."

"I remember the name. But, Jackie, if you knew him, why didn't you identify him for the cops?"

"I don't know. A lot of reasons, I think. That asshole patrolman annoyed me. My ankle hurt me. I didn't want to get involved then. I needed time to think. All of the above."

I threw up my hands, still undecided as to whether I wanted to share more with Matty yet.

I stood up for more coffee and winced as I put weight on my ankle. "Shit. This goddamn ankle hurts."

Matty came right back, as I knew he would, with "Offer it up." We had been taught as children in Good Shepherd to "offer up" pain and annoyances to reduce the time we would spend in Purgatory. Long after I and probably Matty had stopped believing in Purgatory, we had continued the phrase of our childhood.

I wanted to tell Matty the whole story but was worried about implicating him in my "withholding of evidence" or "obstruction of justice."

"Want more coffee?"

"No, I better get back."

Suddenly, I had a way around it." Hang around for a minute. I want to talk to you."

I sat back down at the table and looked into Matty's eyes "Bless me, Father, for I have sinned."

Matty's eyes widened. I had never "gone to confession to him" and I'm sure he knew that I never planned to. Then his face relaxed and he said "Yes?"

"It's been a good while since my last confession, Father, and, recently, I lied to a police officer when I said that I didn't catch the boy I was chasing. Well, actually, he caught me. I fell down the hill on the other side of the field and he came back to help me. He seemed like a good kid. He goes to All Hallows and the Moose just vouched for him. He had a Regents so I let him go."

I held up my hand for my confessor to let me go on. "I didn't volunteer Frankie Ford's name because he called me about two weeks ago. He was in some kind of trouble and seemed to think I could help him."

"I never liked Frankie in All Hallows. He was a bully and a pain in the ass. I embarrassed him in the schoolyard when we were sophomores. He was acting like hot shit on the basketball court until I got on and made him look silly. He tried to get back at me for two years. In the beginning of senior year, he smacked me as he walked by and I got up and hit him just as Brother Carr walked into the room. When Carr dragged us out in the hall, Frankie actually tried to take the blame. I said that it was both our faults. Carr smacked both of us and Frankie and I were ok with each other after that."

"Anyway, I saw him a few times over the years and he seemed to be doing ok, wheeling and dealing on Wall Street. When he called, he first said that he had a computer problem and had lost some data. I started to suggest recovery programs -- Mace or Norton -- but he said that the lost data was only part of the problem and that he needed to talk to me."

"I gave him the address and told him to come over but he told me that he had to go out of town for a while and he'd call me when he got back. Then he turns up dead in the park."

"And when I get home, there's a letter waiting for me from him."

"A letter?"

I got up and got the envelope with the letter and diskette and slid it across the table to Matty as I sat down."

"That's my confession, Father. Any penance?"

"Yes, my son or, rather, brother. One Our Father, Hail Mary, and Glory Be and pray that God makes you more prudent in your actions. Go in peace."

"Prudent? What the hell would you have done differently?"

Matty sighed "Damned if I know. Probably nothing."

"My problem is, other than looking at this disk, what do I do now? Frankie wanted my help but he's dead. I don't even know what killed him."

"He was shot."

"Shot? I didn't see a lot of blood."

"The blood was under his right side -- under his head; you couldn't see it until he was moved. The cops said 'small caliber to the temple'. The bullet's probably lodged in his brain."

"Great. He was probably on his way to my house and somebody shot him before he got here."

Matty thought for a minute. "If it has anything to do with this diskette, I hope that whoever shot him doesn't know where he was going."

"Shit. That's a happy thought."

"Maybe you'd better talk to Jimmy Finn or your state cop friend, Delaney. You said that he handles murder investigations and computer stuff."

"It's out of his jurisdiction and I don't feel like telling Jimmy, at least not just yet, that I lied to the cops. I'm going to sit on it until I look at the disk anyhow."

Matty got up. "Ok. I gotta get back. I hope you know what you're doing."

I stood up with him. "I do too. I'll talk to you later."

As he was going out the door, Matty turned. "By the way, nice move with the seal but it locks me in if anything happens to you."

"Let's not worry about...oh, God!"

"See you" and the door closed behind him.

Chapter 4 – History: Fathers, Beer & Computers

I grew up in the apartment house that I live in now. My parents had moved to Inwood when Matty was one, the year before I was born, My father's partner "on the job," Jack McMullen, had moved to Inwood the year before and my father followed him after a few visits to Jack and Claire's new apartment.

My father and Jack were the closest of friends as well as partners. Jack was my godfather and I was named after him. His son, John, has been my closest friend for as long as I can remember. He is sandwiched between Matty and me, a year younger than one and older than the other. Additionally, he was a year between us at All Hallows and a year ahead of me at Iona.

John was directly responsible for me getting into the computer field. I liked both of his wives very much and, even though he was my best man, he disliked my only wife, Margo, very much. In retrospect, in our judgment of spouses, we were both right.

Another thing that linked us was that we both lost our fathers relatively young. His father died in an accident when he was in grammar school and mine died in a narcotics bust that fell apart when I was a senior in All Hallows, the year after we moved upstairs -- John pointed out that his father died the year after they moved to a larger apartment too.

Another friend, this one in my building, Bob Cummings, lost his father less than a month after mine and the three of us seemed to become even closer after Bob's father passed away.

Matty had already joined the Paulists when our father died. He offered to take a hiatus from his studies and return home until my sister and I finished school but we wouldn't hear of it. Dad's dying "on the job" had left my mother financially secure and there was no shortage of funds for Margaret Mary's and my education.

I majored in accounting and beer drinking at Iona and, upon graduation, was able to obtain a position with Duane & Tweed, one of the "Big Eight" accounting firms. My career took a marked swing when John McMullen parlayed a Department of Defense job into an entry-level position in the computer field and fascinated me with his energy and interest in the new field.

"Jackie, if you have any chance at your firm to move into the computer area, take it. It will be very big."

"But all of our partners come out of the accounting practice. I'd be cutting off my chances for partner."

"Things will change. Take my word. Take a chance."

I did take his word and I did take a chance and he was right.

I read some books about computers and, immediately, knew more about the subject than 95% of the staff at my firm, no matter what their level. When the word came down that we would be establishing a new section to both support our clients and develop a strategy for our internal use of technology, I went right to Franklin Dietz, the partner named to head up the effort, and asked in. It didn't take long for Dietz, a very political animal, to see that he had someone who could wind up carrying the real load while he basked in the glory. I came across as an eager beaver who just wanted to learn and work hard while, actually, I already saw myself in Dietz's job.

I wrote up some fairly detailed analysis of the scope of our new function for Dietz's signature and, while the momentum was still on, I got myself off to IBM's Customer Education Center to learn the tools of my new profession - systems analysis, programming, hardware configurations - I immersed myself in books and materials on computers and business data processing and spent time with our more advanced clients, particularly in the securities industry.

I proposed that Duane & Tweed develop a computerized audit package, becoming the first of the Big Eight to do so. My plan was for us to write the system in conjunction with one of our major securities clients to run on its IBM 7070 computer - the largest business mainframe at the time. We would then be able to use the same system for other clients who had the same basic computer configuration, while writing a new version of the program for our smaller in-house computer system. We could then use our system to run a chargeable audit service for securities firms having different configurations from the IBM 7070. I saw us then writing similar systems for use with our clients in other industries.

Before laying the whole plan on Dietz, I got hold of John, who had coincidentally moved from the Defense Department to our biggest client in the securities industry, Witter & Blyth. I offered him the chance to be the pilot - to help us design the system and be the guinea pig in its use. The advantages to Witter and Blyth would be that it would be in on the ground floor and would have input on the design. It would also mean that it would have to commit resources to the project and John had to go to his superiors to obtain approval to proceed.

John got back to me quickly that the partner in charge of operations at W&B, Bob Flanagan - although I didn't know him, also from Inwood - was interested and wanted a meeting to discuss the proposal further. Now I sprung it on Dietz, taking care to frame it as part of my initial mandate from him; I was just attempting to implement the wonderful plan which he had conceived from the start!

He bought it and asked me to develop a detailed plan, "fleshing out the skeleton," for him to present at the meeting. I did and, by the time I was finished, Dietz understood it well enough to feel comfortable bringing in the audit partner for W&B, briefing him, and getting him to accompany us to the meeting in Flanagan's office.

Dietz reviewed the plan and then deftly deflected questions to me as "the real detail person on the project." Flanagan asked how long I thought the project would take and I soft-shoed a little, saying "We haven't defined the actual requirements yet or established how much technical support that I'd get from W&B. We'd have to do the programming for W&B's 7070 and do all testing on that computer."

Flanagan stopped me. "I'll assign John full time to the project. I assume that you two can work together." Neither Dietz nor the audit partner, Ray Dalrymple, knew of my relationship with John but Flanagan obviously did. He continued, "I want this ready for our next audit and," turning to Dalrymple, "I want a commitment that it will be."

This was a masterstroke on Flanagan's part and could really put me in a box. Audits in the securities industry had to be done on a "surprise" basis with no prior warning. The auditors would just walk in and the audit would begin. Practically, it had to be done on a "month-end" so that the auditors could control the monthly processing of customer statements, inserting a letter with the statement asking the customers to notify the auditors of any errors on the statement. In the case of W&B, because of its size, the audit was normally performed over a three-day weekend to allow our staff more time to complete the counting of securities in order to impact the daily W&B processing as little as possible.

The scheduling of the W&B audit was a major secret within Duane & Tweed, known only to a few partners. The audit required the marshaling of huge resources within our firm for the counting of securities and, hence, was planned months in advance by those few partners. Now Flanagan was asking for a commitment that, no matter what the Duane & Tweed schedule was, there would be no audit until the as-yet-undefined computer system was completed. Smooth!

Dietz walked right in. "Sounds fair to me." I thought Dalrymple would fall off the chair. "I think, Frank, that we better run this by the Executive Committee and then get back to Bob by the end of week, don't you?"

"Well, that will just be a formality, Ray. They've already given me the authority to go ahead with the audit system and it will be great to work with Bob and his staff on this. I'll, of course, run it by the committee but, Bob, why don't we just plan on going ahead? I'm sure we'll produce a great product."

My mind was racing – "A great product, you dummy? You've just put me in an almost no-win situation. I need a working computer system that must be approved by the client before we can audit the client and we have no definition yet. I've never installed a major system and it should have been finished yesterday to protect whatever unknown scheduling has been done by my senior management." I smiled enthusiastically and said "I guess I'll be spending a lot of time here. Is there any place I can work out of here?"

Flanagan said "All set up. There's a desk for you in John's

office with a phone."

As the meeting broke up and I planned to stay around and move in, Ray said "Why don't you walk back with us, Jack? I want to go over some logistics."

As soon as we hit the lobby of Two Broadway, Ray turned to me and said "Can you do this? And right away?" I replied, "We'll have to move quickly with the definition but I'm confident I can." Dietz went to add something but Ray cut him off. "You got us into this, you dopey son of a bitch and you don't even know what you did. You better get Jack any help that he needs and this better get done within three months or you've both got major problems." And Ray walked away.

"Is there a problem getting this done, Jack?"

"I don't know, Frank - but I'll give it everything I have. Don't worry."

"Well I'll be there if you need anything - just let me know."

"Thanks, Frank. It'll work out. I'll go back up to W&B right now and get started."

And it did work out. John and I worked about 100 hours a week and constantly pushed each other. I gathered the definition and wrote the requirements. Flanagan and Dalrymple approved them. John and I designed the system; He did most of the programming while I and a W&B junior programmer wrote a few programs. I designed a testing and acceptance procedure. Dietz would appear regularly to take an active hand but, when Flanagan regularly was too busy to see him, took to giving us a short pep talk and then leaving to "get back for meetings."

A month into the project, Dalrymple called and asked me to lunch in the Harbor View Club, upstairs in Two Broadway. He told me to meet him in the Harbor View lobby at 12:30. When I got to the lobby, Ray was standing there with Jim Elkins, one of our Senior Partners and Vice Chairman of the Executive Committee. Spotting me, Ray said "Jim, here's Jack. You know him, don't you?"

"Sure do, good to see you, Jack" and we shook hands. I didn't think that Elkins would have known me if he tripped over me outside his office.

As we sat down, Ray said "I was briefing Jim on your project, Jack, and I wanted to give you the chance to bring him up to date."

I thought, "Your project? What happened to our project? And where the hell is Dietz?"

I said, "Certainly, Ray. I think we're on target although it is tight. The W&D people have been great but there is a lot of work. I am confident though."

"Ray tells me that you've been putting in a lot of hours, Jack. Can you use some help? Do you want to hire some programmers to take some of the load off you?"

Ray says I've been putting in a lot of hours? How does he know? And do I want to hire some programmers? Since when did I start hiring programmers?

"Funny, I was about to discuss that with Frank, Jim. I'd like to see us hire two top-quality computer people; one to work with me at W&D and the other to start, as we get close to completion at W&D, writing the version for our in-house system. I'm sure you've seen the overall plan that Frank and I put together, Jim, for the Duane & Tweed Computer Audit package; the W&D portion is really just the kick-off of the over-all project."

"I have seen them, Jack, and that's the path that we want to move on - but the most important thing right now is the Witter & Blyth program. It's very important to the firm and I want you to do everything possible to bring it in as rapidly as possible - and I'll give you anything you need to do it. Get a hold of Jim Reardon in Personnel and give him the specs on the people that you want to hire. He'll get you good people and, when you find who you want, I'll approve the hiring - but get any bodies you need to move this project right away."

For the rest of the meal, we talked about the Mets and the Knicks and Princeton, Jim's alma mater. A fellow from Missouri, Bill Bradley, was putting Princeton basketball on the map.

When we left, Ray told Jim that he'd go with me to W&D to

"drop in on Bob." Jim nodded and shook hands with me. "Nice to see you, Jack. Now get the job done for us. I know that you can."

In W&D's lobby, Ray leaned close and said, in a low voice, "I'm going back to the office too. I just wanted to be sure that you understood. You have a wonderful opportunity here - now don't fuck it up."

I assured him that I wouldn't -- And I didn't.

Chapter 5 -- I Call The Cops

Well, back to the story at hand. I had a lot to do even before the morning's events. I was writing a review of the newest release of Paradox for Stan Veit's "Computer Shopper" and had also agreed to do the McMullens' "MacUniverse" column for the same publication while they were away at a conference -- both had deadlines of the next day! I also had to line up speakers for the next few months for "NYPC," the New York IBM Users' Group -- and now I had this goddamn envelope from Ford. I should have put it away until I had completed the work -- I knew that, whatever it was, it would take time and energy.

So I opened it. The envelope contained a floppy diskette and a handwritten note -- a note from a person now dead; more than a little eerie.

I began reading, "Jackie, I'm in a lot of trouble and I don't know what to do. I found a bunch of things that I shouldn't have when doing some work for Billy Norris -- I knew that he was connected but I never realized how deep. I knew that they'd figure out that I had gotten into the files and I'd be in deep shit so I made some floppy disk copies. I kept one, gave one to my cousin Danny, and am sending you this one. It and the others are zipped copies of bigger files. I know that you know a lot about computers and can uncompress the files. Please don't do anything like that until I talk to you. If they catch up to me, I think that I can save myself if I can convince them that there are other copies out there."

"I don't want to give you any problems, Jackie, but I didn't know who else to turn to."

And it was signed "Frankie" -- and he was dead and I had no clue as to whether he had 'given me any problems' or not. Shit!

I sat down at my TeleCompaq - the only failed machine that Compaq ever made but I loved it and did a directory of the diskette. Sure enough, there were three "zipped" files (zipped files are compressed files that must be unzipped to be read by a program. The "unzip" program was known as "pkunzip"). I copied the files to my hard drive, put the floppy back in a disk jacket, and put the jacket inside the cover of "My Turn at Bat" by Ted Williams (my favorite ballplayer) on the next to the top shelf of a bookcase, I folded Frankie's letter and put it in the middle of Peter McWilliams' "The Personal Computer Book" and replaced it on the bottom shelf of the same bookcase.

Frankie had said "Please don't do anything like that until I talk to you" -- well, that wouldn't be for a while -- at least, so I hoped. What to do? I did what I often did when faced with such a quandary -- I went for a ride.

I have two vehicles -- one, a new Honda 250cc Elite Motor Scooter, purchased with the proceeds of three articles for PC Magazine's "Database Shootout," the other, a Volkswagen "bug" that was ostensibly my brother's car so I could park it in the convent parking lot. Parking in Inwood was a real problem, particularly since I didn't use the car every day, so the convent worked out well. Both Matty and I had keys and each of us used the car as needed.

The scooter was my pride and joy and, when I said "I went for a ride," it meant on the scooter. I thought well, or at least I thought I did, when heading up the Taconic State Parkway and over the Bear Mountain Bridge on two wheels.

Actually, I didn't go over the Bear Mt. Bridge -- I headed for it -- The Henry Hudson Parkway into the Saw Mill River Parkway into the Taconic State Parkway -- off at Route 202 -- west to the Bear Mountain Expressway -- but, once I crossed a little bridge and hit the Route 6 / 9 traffic circle, I turned north on Route 9, instead of following 6 to the bridge, and found Route 9D north to the picturesque town of Cold Spring. I parked the scooter in front of the Salmagundi Book Store, a great bookstore with many Hudson River history books. After browsing for about an hour and making the requisite purchase, I was back on the scooter and on the way home -- across Route 301 to the Taconic and then a straight shot south.

I had the scooter for less than a year and had come to motorcycles late. The Inwood that I grew up in was not a car or cycle neighborhood; we walked between the bars or took cabs. Our social life was centered in Inwood Park, the local bars (the most of any neighborhood in New York City), and the local parish, Good Shepherd. The park had basketball courts (the sport of choice), baseball fields, manicured patches of grass on which we kept the card games going, and

New York City's only forest where we drank underage and tried to lure young lovelies, a very difficult task in the pre-pill "let him open your blouse and you go right go hell" days.

I had had my first ride on the back of a scooter when I was about 19 and standing in front of the Pizza Haven on Broadway when "Chuckles" Collins (real first name Bill) pulled up on a scooter and asked if anyone wanted a ride. I jumped on the back and away we went -- this was in the pre-helmet days and, besides it was only a scooter, right? (I also had a body full of beer from McSherry's, next door to the Pizza Haven, so common sense was not at its highest level). We tooled around the neighborhood, went across the Harlem River to Fordham, left on Jerome Avenue, north to the wonderfully steep Kingsbridge Road Hill, west to Broadway, and south back to the Pizza Haven.

By the time the five-mile ride ended, I WANTED one! The fact that I had no money and no driver's license didn't mitigate my hunger but they did mitigate by ability to feed it ... and, by the time I did have the money and the license, the hunger had receded ... only to resurface 25 years later.

The ride settled me; I hadn't realized that the morning activities had caused so much stress but I could feel the calmative effect of the air and the closeness with nature. Unfortunately, though, it did nothing to bring me any closer to an understanding of what I should be doing about the death, young Frankie, or the diskette.

I came up Indian Road and, seeing no one on the sidewalk,

rode onto to it at the driveway of 25 Indian Road and went a half block to the corner of 215th Street – if I hadn't, I would have had to push it up over the curb at the corner. I guided it into the basement and down the baby ramp to the elevator and in. Fortunately, I didn't encounter any other riders; sometime I get nasty looks at the amount of space that my precious scooter takes in the elevator -- and some folks even think that it is weird that I park it in the apartment.

I wiped it down in the hall and brought it into the apartment, guiding it into its own corner. It was time to get to work.

As I sat down to work, firing up a Macintosh to begin writing, I found my mind wandering back to this morning. Finally, in an attempt to resolve some of the questions, I picked up the phone and called the 34th Precinct.

"34th Precinct. Officer Malone."

"Sergeant Finn, please."

"Who's calling?"

"Jack Devine."

After a bunch of clicks, Jim came on the phone. "Jack, I hear you were causing trouble up in the park today -- something about refusing to cooperate with duly constituted authority."

I grinned. He must have learned that expression at the Police Academy and kept it in place until he could pull it on the uninitiated. "Bull shit. Your duly constituted authority acted like a jerk. I come limping across the field like Chester from Gunsmoke after chasing the rabbit that was bending over the poor guy on the ground and he comes on like a storm trooper. The mention of your name calmed him though."

"Yeah, that and the fact that your brother was the attending priest. So you ran after some guy that you saw on the scene?"

"Yes, not one of my brighter moves. I called out 'Hey' when I saw him and the guy on the ground and he took off. Maybe if I hadn't yelled, he wouldn't have run or if I had gotten closer, I might have caught him. As it was, I had no chance -- and then I fell down the goddamned hill."

Jimmy laughed "You wouldn't have fallen 20 years ago."

"No and I might have caught him then."

"You're probably lucky that you didn't. The dead guy took a bullet to the temple - and it was fired from the back. The perp knew what he was doing. You might have been next."

I thought for a minute and then said "Hmmm the kid didn't seem to have a gun. At least, I didn't see one -- and you said that it was from the back. When I saw him, he was lying on his back. Wouldn't he have fallen forward?"

"One thing at a time, It was a small caliber -- a 22 pistol, I think. It could have been in his pocket. Was he wearing a jacket?"

"I don't think so. At least, nothing was flapping around as I chased him, He could have had one of those sweatshirt jackets."

"Ok ... now as to the turning over -- I assume that the kid rolled him over to go through his pockets ... but you must have interrupted him. He didn't get the wallet ... so we could identify him. He's one Francis Ford and he lives in Riverdale."

"Oh shit, Jimmy. That's who I thought it was. I went to high school with him."

Finn's voice took on an edge "Ah, maybe that's why your name, address, and phone number were in his wallet. Why didn't you tell the officers on the scene that you knew the poor son-of-a-bitch?"

He had led me right down the path, probably remembering me eating him up on the basketball courts and delighting in it.

My voice rose a little too. "Why? Because I wasn't sure it was him ... I haven't seen him in over 20 years ... because my ankle hurt like hell ... because your cop acted like a Nazi asshole ... all of the above. That's why I called you now."

He wouldn't be put off "It took you long enough to get to it."

"I move slowly. Now, as to the kid, I didn't see a gun and I didn't see him roll him over. Could it have been someone else?"

"Did you see anyone else?"

I thought for a minute, trying to re-create the picture. "No ... at least, I don't think so."

There was a silence for a moment and then I broke it "Does Frankie have a family?"

"We're trying to check that now. I have a call into the five-oh to see if they know anything. Someone will have to go and interview the wife if there is one."

"Let me know. I'll talk to her."

"I thought you hadn't seen him in over 20 years."

"I haven't, I don't think ... although he may have been at one of our alumni reunions." He was -- I remember talking to him but I let that slide. "But he had my name and number, you said. It must mean that he was planning to look me up ... maybe even today."

"That's what I've been thinking," Jim said, "I'll let you know if anything comes up."

Chapter 6 -- Paradoxes

After I hung up with Jim, I finally got to work. I fired up Paradox and began the testing process. While Paradox had vaulted to the front of the PC-based relational databases due to its innovative use of the "Query-by-Example" ("QBE") interface, its reporting capabilities had left a lot to be desired and this new release was an attempt to correct that.

The McMullens had consulted with Ansa Corporation, the owners of Paradox, on the improvements, so I had to be sure to find some deficiencies to assure myself that I was putting professionalism ahead of friendship. Luckily, that turned out not to be a problem although the new version was far superior to the old, so I wrote the review, printed it, copied it to a floppy, and found a "floppy mailer" to protect the disk as I mailed it off to Stan Veit. We planned to try to deliver the columns by e-mail in the near future but Computer Shopper was not yet ready to accept material in this manner.

Now it was on to the MacUniverse column -- but that required some thought. What was I going to write about. The content of the column was up to the McMullens (or, in this case, me) with the only guideline from Stan being "fifteen hundred interesting words about the Macintosh." As my mind wandered looking for a subject it kept drifting to the other problem -- or problems at hand -- Frank Ford ... the diskette ... Frankie Almonte ... withholding evidence, etc. What was my next move -- both with the column and the murder?

The column answer came first. A friend of mine, Peter Schug, was in the process of re-programming a very rudimentary artificial intelligence personal assistant program that he had written for the TRS-Model 100 to run on the Macintosh. The program, modeled after the persona of Robert Heinlein's "Gay Deceiver" personal flying car and time machine which made wisecracks as it managed Zeb's life (in Heinlein's new "The Number of the Beast"), anticipating his needs. Peter hoped to add audio output and, at some point, input to the system and to build a connection to his Model 100 so that information, things to do lists, phone numbers, etc, could be transferred back and forth. It was a rather ambitious project, although I have no doubt that systems like this will be commonplace in the future. I knew that I could turn the mental outline into an interesting piece for Computer Shopper readers, particularly when I threw in some biographical background on Peter, who made stained glass windows, designed radio controlled airplanes, played odd musical instruments, and had followed the stock market on his Apple II -- all for hobbies.

I concentrated on the task and knocked off the column in about an hour and a half, complete with spell-checking and corrections; I'm a lousy spell-checker and a worse typist. I normally write very fast, once the piece has been "written" in my mind, and I like to think that I write best on deadline -- but that may just be another way of saying that I procrastinate until "push comes to shove."

So, putting that column on a Macintosh formatted-disk and placing the diskette in another mailer for Stan, I was now free to concentrate on the more difficult problem.

Jimmy had said that Frank had been shot by someone who knew what he was doing -- but Frankie's wallet was still in his pocket for Jimmy to find my name and number in it. Was it a robbery? A robbery foiled by the approach of young Frankie? But Frankie didn't mention anyone around Frank when he found him. Did he just not mention it? Or was the killer already gone? And, if it wasn't a robbery, did it have to do with the disk now in my possession? And was I in any danger?

I had to talk to young Frankie -- I obviously couldn't talk to the older one -- and see what was on the diskette -- and push Jimmy on seeing whether Frankie had a wife so I could talk to her. It dawned on me that I shouldn't be thinking any of this. I should be calling Jimmy and telling him the whole story -- giving him young Frankie's name, explaining that he was a good kid and that one of my favorite Irish Christian Brothers had vouched for him and then giving him the diskette and note and letting police do police work. Hell, if there was one thing that my father always said, when snorting at "Mike Barnett, Man Against Crime," was that amateurs should stay out of the way of real police.

That sounded like exactly the right thing to do -- but, then again, both Franks had put their trust in me so, when I reached for the phone thinking I was going to call Jimmy, I found myself dialing 411 and saying "Almonte at 117 Seaman Avenue in Manhattan. Paul Almonte? Yes, That's it. Lorraine 9-0411. Thank you" and before I could regret it, I dialed the number.

A woman with a Spanish accent answered but said, in English, "Hello."

"Hello, is Franklin in?"

"Yes but he's studying. Please don't keep him too long. Frankie … phone."

A minute later, he came on the phone "Hello."

"Frankie, this is Jack Devine. We met in the park today."

His voice changed immediately with apprehension creeping in. "Yes. Brother Sullivan told me that you called." The question hung in the air.

"I didn't tell him anything about the chase or the dead person -- just that I ran into you in the park. Have you said anything to your parents?"

A pause "No, that wouldn't be a good idea."

"Ok. Get a pen and take down my number. I'm a friend of Brother Sullivan's and he recommended you as someone who could run some errands for me. Will that work? I need some answers."

"Yeah. That should be ok. What's the number?"

"LO7-6004. Did you see anyone else around the body? ... anyone at all?"

"LO 7?"

"6004. Did you see anything?"

"No, I'm sure that I didn't. But I should go. Can I call you some other time? My mother is really on me about studying."

"Sure. Go ahead. Call me when you can. Good luck on the tests."

"Thanks," and he was gone.

I went to the refrigerator and got a Pepsi and sat in front of the computer, trying to get up the energy to get involved in the zipped files. It was 11:30 and I knew that, once I started, I'd be on for hours. I finished the Pepsi, turned out the lights, went into the bedroom and turned on Johnny Carson. By the time the monologue was over, I was finished too. I turned off the light and went to sleep. It had been a very long day.

Offering It Up

Chapter 7 -- The Letter

The phone rang about 3AM. Years of being involved with computer implementations had conditioned me to come instantly awake. I had been off that track for a few years but I still woke up immediately and grabbed the phone.

"Hello?"

A gruff voice "Did Frank Ford give you anything?"

I feigned sleep "Who? Who is this?"

The gruff voice got cold "I asked you a fuckin' question. Did Ford give you anything?"

I responded in kind. "Who the fuck is Ford? ... and it's three o'clock in the fucking morning? Who are you calling? Are you drunk?"

"Ok. You may be on the level or you may not be. You may hear from me again." Click.

Shit. Now I had to get up and get on those files and see just how much jeopardy I might be in.

I rolled out of bed, grabbed a shirt and a pair of Bermudas, went to the "computer room," turned on the lights, started both the Mac and TeleCompaq booting, and went out to the kitchen to start coffee. What the fuck had I gotten myself into? I should just gather up the disk and letter and get myself down to the 34th Pct. and get myself out of it. But that would mean still having to cover for the kid. Well, I could do that -- but Frankie had been looking for my help! So what? I'm a computer person -- an accountant -- a basketball junkie -- all of those -- but not a cop -- and certainly not Mike Hammer. My reverie was interrupted by the coffeemaker finishing. I poured a cup three-quarters full, topped it with half-and-half, and went back to the computers to see what Frankie had laid on me.

There were three zip files on the TeleCompaq, "readme.zip," "nyent.zip," and "nortrad.zip." Before beginning, I set up a directory, "ff" to place the files in. When I was finished, I would go in and hide the directory from any prying eyes that might arrive. I assumed that he wanted me to begin with the "readme.zip" file so I did, unzipping it to the ff directory.

There had been three files in the package -- two with .doc extensions, obviously Microsoft Word files, and one with a .wks, obviously a 1-2-3 spreadsheet. I brought up Microsoft Word opened the file "readme.doc." A note from Frankie filled the screen and I began to read, scrolling down as I did.

"Jackie,

If you're reading this without me with you, I'm either dead or have been caught by Bill Norris' guys and probably will be dead. Bill's from downtown -- the Westside -- and went to Manhattan with me. He was an operator even then -- but very bright and did well in Finance even though he was always in the Pinewood in a back booth -- I think he might have been running a book while he was in college. I didn't see him for a few years after graduation but then one day I ran into him in the lobby of Two Broadway. He gave me a big wave and told me that he was with Drexel Burnham in the Arbitrage area and doing real well. I was still with Reynolds then in Two Broadway. He was on his way to his office on Broad and Beaver and was just cutting through Two Broadway. We exchanged numbers and agreed to meet for lunch.

I was in Personnel at Reynolds and was going at night to NYU for an MBA. I know that I was a wiseass at All Hallows but college straightened me out. I was also seeing a nice girl, Kathy McCullough. I met her in your old neighborhood at the Inwood Lounge.

Anyway, Billy and I met a lot after that for lunch, usually in Busto's before it closed. He had moved up to Martinis by then, although he never showed it, and seemed to be flush with money. He was always in a hurry to get back to the office. He was good company but you could almost feel a dark side to him; you could always tell that he had some kind of side deals going on that be couldn't talk about.

Anyway, the more prosperous he seemed to get, the more hyper he became. Finally, he told me that he was going to leave Drexel and go off on his own. He said that he'd be able to do much better and that he wouldn't have people looking over his shoulder all the time.

He left Drexel and took his own office right in Two Broadway under the name of Manhattan Equities -- nice space and much more than he needed. So I used to drop down at lunchtime with Zum Zum takeout and we'd eat. He seemed always on the go, even more hyper.

Then, when Reynolds was being gobbled up by Dean Witter and I was about to put the resume out, he offered me a job. He said that his books were getting out of control and he needed someone that he could trust to straighten them out -- and he offered me twenty grand more than I was making. So I took the job and it turned out to be the worst decision I ever made.

I needed the job; Kathy was pregnant with our second – [Damn, I wonder if his wife is in danger. How do I get a hold of her? Shit, Frankie -- what have you gotten me involved with?] -- and we had just bought a house in Bardonia so I couldn't afford to be on the street.

Of course, the goddamn job wound up destroying my marriage but I couldn't have know that then. I had a lot to do to get Billy organized, especially since some of his in-and-out transactions seemed to clearly violate SEC rules, When I pointed it out to him, he said "Relax, Frankie. Everyone does it -- and that's why you're here -- to keep me straight or, at least, to cover my ass when I'm not."

Well, it became more and more covering his ass than anything else and, as he made more and more, he was cutting me in for a piece and the conscience was more and more turned off. Billy was feeding money to people all over for inside tips and was making a bundle from the tips -- a clear violation of insider trading regulations. He seemed to have sources all over the place -- in companies, in brokerage firms, in the financial press -- and they all came through for him.

A bunch of the contacts with these folk involved dinners -- if he could be seen in public with the source -- or at bars all over if he couldn't -- and I went along to 'watch his back'. I was out more and more nights and drinking more and more and it tore my marriage to hell.

The size of our client portfolios began to grow too. Lots of money moved through our books. I never met any of the clients but they all seemed very well off and they had to be happy with the money that Billy was making for them, or so I thought.

I found out over the next few years that the profits were only incidental to most of the clients and that the money movement was the most important thing. The clients were the mob -- Bill Napoli and his buddies -- and we were laundering money and, worst of all, I was getting in deeper and deeper.

I spent a lot of time looking for ways for our transactions to bear legal scrutiny, should it come to that-- and, as I did, I worried more and more -- and, as I worried, I drank more and more, often out with Billy much of the night and, sometimes, there were women involved -- women who wanted to please Billy and me. It was no wonder Kathy finally packed up and left.

When she left, I really hit bottom emotionally but I kept getting deeper and deeper with Billy, He came to me one day and said "Frankie, it looks like the heat is going to come on. There are all sorts of investigations that may come along. You gotta protect me ,.. protect us. Make sure that we have the books set up so we're legitimate ... but keep another so we have our own hammer."

Our own hammer? What the hell was he talking about? But I didn't want to ask so I just went and did it. What you have here are copies of the public books and the real books -- but I'm getting ahead of myself.

Things kept moving along -- more money for me and more women -- but my drinking slowed as I saw Billy getting more frazzled. I missed Kathy. Besides, the stories about investigations into our clients for drugs and murder was scaring the hell out of me -- drugs?

murder? What the hell was I doing?

Finally, I went to Billy and told him that I couldn't take it any more. I was leaving and I suggested that he close it up too before we went to prison -- before I did, I made these copies just in case I had trouble.

Billy went ballistic "Leave? What are you, fucking crazy? You can't leave and neither can I. I'm just a fucking employee, don't you know that? These fucking goombahs own me -- and they own you too. If you try to leave, you go from being an employee to being a loose-end -- you probably know what happens to loose-end, Frankie."

"You think I like this, Frankie? I'm as scared shitless as you are. The day that I become a liability, I'm gone … gone … D-E-A-D … gone."

I'd never seen Billy like this. He was always so self-assured -- and, if he had this much to fear, I knew I was in deep shit. I also knew that he'd give me up if he had to protect himself; hell, he might give me up just to make himself look good, whether to the cops or to our customers, our masters.

I had already smuggled the disks out so, when I finally got out of the office and home, I made some copies. I was going to send one set to Kathy but decided that I better keep her well out of it and then I thought of you. I still had your address from the last All Hallows reunion.

PS. I still wasn't sure if I was going to send this to you but, when I called Billy this morning to say I was taking a day off, he sounded hysterical and told me to get in right away. I'll mail these on the way in.

Most of the money coming in to the real books is dope money -- maybe some prostitution and gambling. So be careful with this stuff; I don't want you in trouble too.

"Thanks, Frank."

So now he was dead and I had material that some mob guys -- the guys who probably killed him -- were after me. Swell!

Chapter 8 -- Call For The FBI

It was 6 AM by now. Time goes fast when you're having fun. I had to do something to get this monkey off my back. I had to get control of the situation, - right now. The dead Frank and the scary guy on the phone were in control; it was time for me to take charge. I poured another cup of coffee and, then, at exactly 6:45 called Joe Conway, my friend and personal FBI agent. I've known Joe since he was in his senior year in high school and came down from Marble Hill to hang around in Inwood. After graduating from Manhattan Prep, Joe had stayed local and gone to Manhattan College and then followed many Inwoodites by going directly into the FBI.

He answered the phone "Yes?"

"Joe, its Jackie Devine. I've got a problem."

"Of course you have. Why else would you be calling me at this ungodly hour?"

I let that slide, knowing that Joe had already been out running in Central Park, and explained the whole story from beginning to end.

Joe just listened and, when I was finished, said "Ok, I believe that we have an ongoing investigation connected to this. Here's what I want you to do. Do you have a Xerox?"

"Yes."

"Make a few copies of what you have. Put one in an envelope and mail it to me. Can you make copies of those diskette things?"

Joe wasn't the most technically literate person I knew. "Yes. Sure."

"Ok put them in the envelope and mail them to me." He gave me the FBI address. Now, put another set of everything in an envelope and meet me in McSherry's about 11 and I'll go over what you have and take it back with me. Make another copy for yourself. Do you have any place out of the apartment that you can put it? I don't want you to leave any of it in the apartment. Then I want you to get out of there. I don't want to panic you but there many be some bad folks coming to visit you soon."

That was all I needed to hear. I spent the next hour doing just as Joe directed. I hedged it slightly by keeping two sets for myself, one in my hiding place and one re-sealed in plain sight by the computer – I hoped that any intruder would be satisfied with what he might feel was the original un-opened package.

I packed the packages to be delivered or mailed into the trunk of my scooter and threw a light jacket in with them, locked the door and pushed my scooter down the hall and into the elevator. As the elevator passed the first floor on its way to the basement, I saw three very tough and unsavory men waiting to go up. While realizing that I might be overreacting to the phone call, I held the door in the basement until I had the scooter started and then rode out of the basement.

As I rode out to turn right on Indian Road, I looked up the hill and saw another stranger, also tough looking, leaning on a late model Lincoln. I turned right onto Indian Road, another right onto 218th Street, right on Seaman Avenue, down Seaman to 207th Street, left on 207th, another left on Cooper Street, and straight onto Park Terrace West, all the time looking over my shoulder to see if the Lincoln was following me.

When I stopped on the corner of Park Terrace West and 215th and looked down the two blocks to the front of my house, I saw the Lincoln still parked in front of my house, confirming that I had not been followed. I parked the scooter and searched in the trunk for a small pair of binoculars. Taking them out, I leaned against the building and focused on the license plate of the Lincoln; it was a New Jersey plate, 1GBD74. I noted the plate on a pad and continued to watch.

About 45 minutes later, two of the three heavies came down the steps to the Lincoln -- and one of them was carrying my computer! I put the glasses down and went across the street to a pay phone and called McSherry's; Joe was already there. I told him what had happened and gave him the plate number. He told me to stay where I was and that he'd be up in a few minutes "with some reinforcements."

I kept watching but nothing else of interest happened until a plain blue Ford pulled up next to me with Jim Finn driving, Sgt. Joe McKenna next to him and Joe in the back seat. "I see you brought the cavalry," I said to Joe. "Thanks for coming, Jim, Joe."

Jim said "The FBI guy told us that it was a big collar. Too big for the FBI. Is there still one in the apartment?"

"Yeah, I think so."

"Ok. Then give us 5 minutes to get down to Indian Road and park the car. Is there a door out to that back alley?"

"I think it's locked."

"That'll be ok. When you see Joe in your doorway, ride down the hill and into the basement – you park the scooter there, right?"

"Actually, I take it up to the apartment on the elevator."

"Better. Ride down as normal and put it on the elevator and take it upstairs as normal. You'll see us around – but don't talk to us. Got it?"

I nodded and, before they drove away, I gave Joe the package with Frankie's material.

Chapter 9 -- An Arrest In My Apartment

I waited for what seemed to be a very long 12 minutes – I didn't want the guys who had stolen my computer to just disappear – until I saw Joe in my doorway. I started up the scooter and rode down 215th Street. By the time I got to my basement entrance, Joe was gone. I pushed the scooter down to the elevator and pressed the button. When it arrived, Jimmy was on it. He whispered "Give me your apartment key." I did and as we approached six, he whispered again "Stay in the elevator."

When the elevator stopped, Jim opened the door and began to push the bike down the hall. Not heeding his most recent admonition, I stepped out and flattened against the wall to watch. Joe McKenna was flattened against the wall on the second step of the stairway to the roof and had his gun drawn. Jim held the scooter up with his body, opened the door with the key, and pushed in, just as I would have. I heard a voice. "Park the bike and close the door, and you won't get hurt." As the last of the words reached me, McKenna jumped into the room, yelling "Police! Put the gun down and get on the floor. NOW!"

Without thinking, I ran down the hall to the apartment, entering right behind Conway who also had a drawn gun. Finn was holding the tough guy from behind while McKenna picked up the dropped gun. The scooter had fallen against the table and I righted it and wheeled it away as Finn said "I thought I told you to stay in the elevator."

"You're in my apartment. I wanted to straighten up."

Joe McKenna handed Finn a pair of handcuffs and, as Jim cuffed the unwelcome visitor, McKenna said "You're under arrest for breaking and entering, grand larceny, attempted murder, and resisting arrest" and began the Miranda litany. For the first time, the hood spoke, "Attempted murder? What a crock." Joe Conway spoke for the first time, "You were in this apartment, waiting for this gentleman with a drawn gun. Obviously, your intention was to kill him."

"Who the fuck are you?" the hood growled at Joe. Joe flashed the badge 'FBI, Tommy, and when these gentlemen are through with you, you and I will have some business to discuss."

As "Tommy" shut up and listened to McKenna finish the Miranda, I wondered where the "Tommy" came from. Joe's calling him by name had obviously had an effect as Tommy said not another word.

When McKenna finished the Miranda, Jim searched Tommy's pockets and lifted a wallet out of his back pocket. He flipped through it 'The driver's license says "Albert Walker." We all looked at Joe.

"His real name is Tommy Napoli and he's wanted for murder in Chicago. When Jackie called and mentioned Frank Ford and Bill Norris in his story, Norris' name rang a bell so I checked out the known associates of Norris and came up with a bunch of bad characters. One is Bill Napoli, Tommy's cousin. Looking at the family, I came across this scumbag. He was muscle for a loan shark in Chicago and muscled too hard on one poor SO, in front of witnesses. This dumb son-of-a-bitch must have moved here as soon as the warrant went out. Obviously, his choice of friends and occupation hasn't changed."

Bill Napoli? His name was in Frankie's note.

I watched this Napoli as Joe talked – all of the fight seemed to have gone out of him. "What the fuck were you doing in my apartment? – and where's my computer."

Napoli didn't say a word but Joe answered for him. "Tommy's going to think it over in jail and will realize that, if we don't help him, he's either away for life or gets the plug pulled on him in Chicago; Illinois still has the death penalty. The citizen that this schnook killed was a school teacher and Little League coach. No matter if he had a gambling problem or not, he was a solid citizen and his murderer is a prime candidate for the immediate afterlife."

While Joe talked, Joe McKenna was on the phone. When he hung up, he said, "A couple of uniforms are on the way over to pick up this trash. I think we have some work to do here after he leaves." Jim and Joe just nodded.

Offering It Up

Chapter 10 -- I Come Clean

Within ten minutes, two uniformed officers arrived and took Napoli. I said, "I'll make some coffee" but Joe interrupted me, putting his hand up and then his finger to his lips. "I have to take you down to my office and NYPD here has to go catch criminals." As Joe led us out, I stopped to lock the door but, after this morning's happenings, wondered what good I was doing.

In the elevator, Joe said "Those guys were in your house for a couple of hours. They may have planted bugs. I'll have someone come up and check it out. Do you have an extra key with you?" As it happened, I carried two key rings – a result of many self-imposed lockouts – and handed him a key. Joe continued "I really do want to have a talk with all of us – let's go into the playground."

As soon as we had settled, Jim, who had been fairly quiet since the initial entry into the apartment, turned to me. "Joe mentioned Frank Ford, the guy that was killed yesterday. You seem to know a lot more about Ford and his friends than you did when you talked to me last night."

I blanched. I felt badly that I hadn't totally leveled with Jimmy and he had just risked his life for me. "I didn't know a lot last night. When I checked my mail, there was a note from Frank and a computer diskette. I put it all away until I finished some work and then was too tired to bother. I went to bed, planning to look it at this morning, but that changed when some rat bastard woke me up in the middle of the night threatening me on the phone. I thought I had put him off, but it's obvious from the appearance of Tommy and friends that I didn't."

Jimmy seemed more interested than angry so I went on. "I got up and looked at the diskettes and Frankie's notes. The materials on the diskette look like the records of some kind of money laundering operation, or, at least, some kind of tax fraud. It sounded federal to me so I called Joe this morning and he told me to meet him at McSherry's with the stuff. He also told me to get the hell out of the apartment and it's obviously a good thing that I did."

"So the kid you chased probably had nothing to do with the murder."

I decided to open up all the way "No, he's a good kid. He was trying to help Frankie. He saw him lying there and was bending over him when I yelled. He took off then. He goes to All Hallows and a brother there, an old friend, vouched for him."

"So you did catch him." The edge in the voice was back.

"No, actually, he caught me. When I fell on my ass on the hill, he came back to help me. He was out for a run before a Regent's. I figured that he wouldn't have come back to help me if he was the bad guy. So I told him to go take his Regents."

"Does anybody else know that you weren't level with the police on the scene?"

"Just you guys here – and my confessor – and he can't say anything."

Jimmy finally grinned. "Jesus, you brought Matty into your criminal obstruction."

Joe broke in. "Can we get back to this later, Jim? I'd bet that Tommy or one of his buddies was Ford's killer. Now Jackie, and maybe Ford's ex-wife, are in danger. If Norris thinks that they have information that can fry him, he'll want to get rid of them. We don't have anything solid on Norris yet but Tommy may help us there."

Joe went on. "I'll bet Norris is panicking right now – and not just because of us. He's probably laundering for some much bigger fish. Just as Ford was a danger to him, he's a real danger to whoever he's involved with -- Napoli or even the Columbians, Mafia, or the Russians. If the word gets out that we're on to him, he immediately becomes very expendable to those folk, and he knows it."

Joe McKenna nodded "Ok. What's next?"

"Ok", Joe started, "there is a lot we can do today. Jackie, can we put a tap on your phone?"

"Certainly."

"Ok. I'll also arrange to have your apartment swept for bugs. I'm sure that those gibronies planted some while they were there. That's why I needed a key."

Joe turned to Jim, "Can you park a plain clothes in the area today until tonight? I'll move in and stay over tonight. Is that ok, Jackie?"

I nodded and Jim said "I'll see what I can do. I'll have to talk to the commander when I get back."

Joe said "I'll make a call if you think it will help."

Jim shook his head "I'll handle it. If I have a problem, I'll give you a call."

Joe nodded and turned to me "Now, I'd like you to get on that scooter and go on a long ride so we can get set up. I don't want you in that apartment until we have the place swept, tap set up, and on-going protection."

"Hmmm. Does that mean I'm in danger?"

"It's possible. Did your visitors get anything they were looking for?"

I shook my head. "I don't think so. I erased the files from the hard disk on the computer that they took and I gave the floppies to you."

"So, they may be back – or they may try to put some pressure on you in another way. I don't think your children are in any jeopardy but I'd talk to your ex-wife and find out who the local law enforcement is. I'll give them a call."

"My kids could be in danger?"

"Calm down. I don't think so – but let's just touch all the bases."

Despite his protestations, I was now concerned.

Offering It Up

Chapter 11 -- Guinan's

I took Joe's directions seriously and went up stairs and began to pack the scooter. I packed a rain jacket, a few books – Andrew Greeley's latest novel, Stephen King's latest and Peter McWilliams' "The Personal Computer Book" and a couple of underwear changes, just in case. I also thought about calling Margo and mentioning the low-probability chance of danger to her, John, and Becky – but decided against it. They were living outside of Pittsburgh and I felt that both the distance and her new name, Travers, made it unlikely that such a call was worth the alarm to her and aggravation to me.

I locked the apartment – although that had done little good against the first bunch – and took the scooter down in the elevator and hit the road. I went down Indian Road to 218th Street, over to Broadway and left across the 225th Street Bridge, left on 228th Street and over to Kingsdale Esso where I stopped to fill the tank. Jimmy, one of the owners, and a very friendly man, looked at the scooter and said "Great wheels. Nice day for a ride, huh? Where are you taking it?"

"Up toward Cold Spring. I really like that town."

"It's nice up there. You should stop in Garrison. Leo says that the area down by the station where they hold the Arts Festival is great." Leo was Jimmy's partner in Kingsdale.

"Thanks, maybe I will." I paid Jimmy and I was off, up the

Riverdale hill and onto the Henry Hudson Parkway heading toward the Saw Mill River Parkway and the Taconic State, all two lane highways going through beautiful New York State scenery.

As I rode, my mind drifted. In just a few days, my whole life had been disrupted. A murder, a threat, me playing cops and robbers with the FBI and NYPD, and, now a "Get out of Dodge" warning from Joe. I was probably more used to change than most – going through marriage, career change, parenting, divorce, death of those near to me, and becoming an independent consultant – but this was ridiculous.

I got off the Taconic at Route 202, picked up the Bear Mountain Expressway to Route 9, and headed north. Following my usual path, I turned east off 403 to 9D, the route to Cold Spring but, rather than turning on 9D, I remembered Jimmy's recommendation and crossed 9D to what became Lower Station Road and followed the road across a bridge over the train tracks to a parking area by the Garrison Railroad Station. I parked the scooter, locked my helmet to it, and walked through a little area of stores, an art gallery, a rare book store, and a train station. As I walked toward the station, the area on my right opened and I saw a magnificent view of the Hudson River. There was a little marina on the Garrison side and dialogically across the river, a little to the north, was the towering structure of the United States Military Academy at West Point. The late spring beauty of the scene was breathtaking.

At the very end of the street, overlooking the marina was

what looked like a private house that also contained a little delicatessen. In front of the open store door were tables and chairs. It looked liked a lovely place to stop and have a sandwich and a soda.

I walked through the door into a narrow store aisle with a deli counter on my right and milk and soda cases on my left. The end of the aisle, surprisingly, opened into a room with a little bar and a short white-haired man on a stool behind it. I walked into the room and saw that it was glass to both the east and south and had a marvelous view of the Hudson. The man said "Welcome. Can I give you a beer?" I thought about it for a second and said "No. I better have a soda. I'm driving a motor scooter." He nodded and said "Coke?"

I took the bottle of Coke, paid him and took a seat at the bar. He reached his hand across the bar. 'Jim Guinan."

"Jackie Devine. This is some great view. Is it your place?"

He nodded "Yes. My wife Peg and I run it. Are you just passing through?"

"I live on the northern tip of Manhattan Island, Inwood, but ride up here fairly often. I have friends in Yorktown, Jefferson Valley, really, and I really like Cold Spring. It's the first time I've been here, though. You have a beautiful location."

"Thank you. Stop in on us often. We have a nice bunch of people here. You'll enjoy it here."

Offering It Up

Jim was obviously a very nice person and was well used to greeting people. He reminded me somewhat of a much smaller version of my favorite bartender in Inwood, Pat Gallagher in the Broadstone. "Thank you. I'll be sure to do that."

Jim smiled, "And from the looks of you, you might enjoy 'Irish Night'."

"Irish Night?"

"Yes. On the first Thursday following every full moon, musicians from around the Hudson Valley come and play – we generally have a few hundred people listening outside during the summer and about fifty in here during the winter."

I looked around the room, thinking, "Fifty? Where does he fit them?"

"When is the next full moon and what time do you start?"

"It's a week from tonight and we start about eight o'clock. I hope that you come up. I think you'll enjoy it."

"Thank you. I'll try to."

Others began to drift in and I moved to a stool at the far end of the bar and watched the boats go by on the Hudson. The conversation, as in most bars I had spent time in, and I spent a lot of time in the Inwood bars, dealt with sports and persons in the neighborhood but also had a river flavor with talk of canoes and kayaks as well as the larger boats in the marina.

Inwood, supposedly, had more bars than any other neighborhood in New York City and, while this may or many not have been true, I had no reason to doubt it. While I drank very little now and was actually thinking of giving it up altogether, I had over the years in Inwood hung out at various times in Erin's Isle, The Willow Tree, The Broadstone, Grippo's Torch Café, Bowl-a-rama Cassidy's, and Minogue's – usually with the same group of friends; we moved from haunt to haunt for various reasons. I also spent many summer evenings in Rockaway, trying to pick up young ladies in the Leitrim Castle or, more productively, listening to Ruthie Morrissey singing songs of the revolution in Mickey Carton's Mayo House across the street.

In the Irish Catholic / Jewish neighborhood of Inwood in the "pre-pill days" where the Catholic girls, through the constant admonitions of nuns, thought that if you opened your blouse you would both get instantly pregnant and doomed to the fires of hell, our male hormones got their only release through sports, drinking, and an occasional fight.

In addition to the plethora of bars, Inwood Hill Park, a massive park, complete with the only forest in New York City, was available to us for underage and summer drinking. There was always some deli that would sell to us "for our parents" or some of-age person who would buy for us. It might be some compassionate soul who has just gone through our underage years or some adult, such as "Bernie the Bum," looking to turn a profit from the kids. "Yeah, Old Mr. Boston Lemon Flavored Vodka went up seventy-five cents." We knew better but why argue? Since the legal age of drinking in New York State is 18, most of us had our first beers at 14 or 15 and, so when we could finally get served in bars, often underage, we "were ready." Now, years later, many of the folks I grew up with have fallen into the bottle, gone into a twelve step program, or like me, cut way back on drinking. Once I went into the consulting business, I stopped drinking at lunch. Although I had a large capacity and never felt that a few beers impaired my afternoons, no client would know that and the smell of alcohol on my breath could make them feel that they weren't getting 100% for their money. This was one of the things that John had passed on when I was going out on my own; he and Barbara had had their own business for a few years and had encouraged me to become my own boss. After listening to them for a while, I did follow their advice; my mother had just gotten sick and I needed some flexibility with hours so I cashed in my profit-sharing, resigned what had become a very lucrative position as the Partner in Charge of Computer Systems and Development at Duane & Tweed, and went off on my own.

It took a while to get used to not having a secretary to type, get me ten cups of coffee a day, keep my appointments straight, and keep me organized, but I slowly got used to it. Some of my old D&W contacts gave me work and the McMullens sub-contracted some while getting me immersed in the burgeoning world of personal computers. It turned out that I had gone on my own at just the right time. The personal computer explosion had business constantly reaching out for expertise and my plate was full all the time.

My reverie was broken by the realization that the sun was starting to set across the Hudson and that I had no clue what I would be doing when I left Guinan's. Was I going home or finding a place to spend the night? I caught Jim's attention, "Are there hotels in the area – or motels?"

Jim thought for a second. "Well, if you go south, there's the Peekskill Motor Inn. That's supposed to be nice. If you go north on 9D, Plumbush's has a Bed and Breakfast. It's probably expensive because the dinners are dear. On you could keep going north to Fishkill or even Poughkeepsie. There are plenty of motels along Route 9 but, if you're going to go that far, you may want to get on your scooter before it gets too dark."

I decided to call Joe before I made up my mind and, after getting a pocketful of change, went out to the pay phone outside the deli. Luckily, I got through the FBI phone morass and caught him at his desk. "Jackie, where are you?"

"I'm up in Garrison, New York and trying to figure out if I'm going home or finding a place."

"I think it's better if you stay away for a day. I'm told that the stuff on those diskettes is hot and we want to be sure that we have everything in place before we use you as bait."

"Bait? Are you nuts? What makes you think I want to be

bait?"

"I don't think you have much of a choice. These guys probably won't get off your case until we lock them up and them coming after you gives us the best chance of locking them up."

"Great „. just fucking great. Why will tomorrow be better for me to come home than today?"

"We want to get the phones and place totally wired and to put in an emergency button for you to push. We'll hide it someplace out of the way and, if something happens that we haven't prepared for, we'll have an emergency fall-back for you. You'll be alright."

I was not convinced but it sounded better than just having those guys show up with no protection at all. "Ok … if you say so, but I'm making you responsible for my life."

"Another thing – we want to have Kevin Reilly stay in your apartment tonight instead of me. Tommy Napoli and I are spending some time getting to know each other and it may go late. You know Kevin. He says he went to All Hallows and Iona with you."

"Sure, but I didn't even know that he was in the FBI; the last I heard of him, he was coaching basketball at All Hallows. He was a year behind me. He was in Artie Burns' year at Iona. Are you sure you need someone there? I won't even be home."

"Just to make sure that, if those guys call or come back before we're ready to have you there, we have an answer for them."

This still didn't sound good. "Ok, give my regards to Kevin. I better call Matty to make sure that he doesn't drop in. Do you think he's in any danger?"

"No, I doubt they even know about him. I wouldn't worry him. Call me tomorrow before you come home. If you can't get me here, call your apartment. Somebody will be there."

I called Matty at the rectory and, when he wasn't there, I left a message that I had taken a ride and was staying overnight upstate as I was too tired to scooter home. I thought that when he got the message he might think I got lucky.

Sidebar -- "Guinan's"

Guinan's, a country store and barroom, located over the Hudson River in the Garrison, New York train station for over 40 years (it has since closed following the death of its founder, **Jim Guinan**, and his son, **John**, who managed the place in later years) is best understood by reading **Gwendolyn Bounds**' wonderful book, "the little chapel on the river," which details the interlocking history of the family, the store, and the town.

One of long-standing traditions at Guinan's was the assemblage of musicians from all over the Hudson Valley on the Thursday most immediately following a full moon to play well into the night for the often hundreds of citizens who would come to listen, sing along, and schmooze. These festivals were called both "Irish Night" and "The Rising of The Moon."

My experiences at these festivals is described in the following poem:

The Communion of Saints
By johnmac the bard

It's Irish Night at Guinan's
first Thursday after the full moon
and the place is packed.

And there is a harp
And a bodhrán
And a few accordions
And a whistle
And a few guitars
And a few fiddles
And some singers
And a lot of beer.

There are some writers
And plumbers
And a Governor
(with a State Police Guard)
And restaurateurs
And real estate agents
And professors
And whoever else walks in.

And there is much talk and gaiety
until there is a hush when
Jim is ready to sing
 "I'll Take You Home Again, Kathleen"
And we all listen.

Kelly's behind the bar
Jim's in the kitchen
And we all take turns
putting the money on
the deli register.

Trust abounds, laughter is king,
joy reigns, and we are friends
with people we don't even know.

And then it ends
And we all go home.
We are a funny people.

Chapter 12 -- Overnight In Cold Spring

I decided to head north. I had passed Plumbush's a number of times when riding to Cold Spring and decided to stay there; it was a building on a large property on Route 9 and had both a restaurant and a bed-and-breakfast within a large old building. I said goodbye to Jim, promising to return whenever I could, fired up the scooter, and went on my way.

I pulled into Plumbush's lot and, although I may have looked strange with no luggage, registered with no trouble and was shown to a room on the second floor. I had planned to go into Cold Spring to eat and pick up a change of underwear but, after lying down to read for a while, I went out like a light. This whole craziness must have exhausted me more than I realized. I woke up about midnight to go to the bathroom – it was a good thing I was still dressed; the common bathroom was down the hall. When I returned from my midnight run, I read for another hour and then it was back to sleep again.

When the sun woke me up in the morning, I felt a little roachy but was reluctant to take a shower in the common bathroom and decided to wait until I got home – and then realized that I didn't know when I would be going home. I had no idea how I would get my work done with no computers. The goons had taken both my Compaq and my Mac and, while all my files were backed up and the floppies hadn't been taken, I had nothing to put the floppies in. This required immediate attention but only if the attention wouldn't put my life in jeopardy.

I could probably get my diskettes and come back up to the McMullens' and use their equipment but, if it were too unsafe for me to be home, I wouldn't want to take a chance on bringing my jeopardy with me to their house.

Pulling on my clothes again, I decided to have breakfast at Plumbush's and then ride into Cold Spring and call Joe. At least I could find out if I could go home. I'd worry about the rest then.

Plumbush's provided a country breakfast – eggs and meat – and when I didn't jump at the scrambled eggs – which I hate – the head waiter insisted on having an omelet prepared for me. While the omelet, bacon and sausage were very good, the orange juice and three cups of coffee were what really got me going. I finished up, paid the bill with my Diner's Club card, and headed toward Cold Spring.

Stopping at the first gas station to fill my beauty up, I called Joe. Joe was away from his desk someplace but I got to speak to Kevin Reilly who was back from my apartment already. Kevin had played ball with me both at All Hallows and Iona – or, rather, I played with Kevin. He was one of the team's stars from the get go while I really hit my stride at the end of my college career and in various Wall Street leagues. Kevin was about 5'8' tall, a tough red-headed sparkplug who could shoot the eyes out of the basket, although Iona coach Jimmy McDermott's methodical style of play normally didn't allow Kevin to shoot much. I can still hear Jimmy screaming "You're my playmaker, dammit! Move the ball." Kevin had coached for a few years at Power Memorial.

John's brother was the principal of Power and hired Kevin. He'd gone on to coach at our alma mater, All Hallows, and was rumored to be the eventual successor to McDermott at Iona. However, as he told me, he left coaching for a variety of reasons, and turned to the FBI instead and was now working out of the New York office. After talking for a while about what Kevin said was an uneventful night at my house, I said that I'd call Joe back in about an hour and went off to Cold Spring to kill some time.

Cold Spring is a beautiful little town and I wandered up and down the main drag, looking in the windows of the antique and art shops until I settled in at the Salmagundi book store. I tend to hang around in bookstores anyhow. "Paperbacks Plus" in Riverdale is a favorite but Salmagundi is especially warm. I found one of Upton Sinclair's "Lanny Budd" novels in the stacks and this made my day.

The day improved further when I called Joe from a phone in the train station and was informed that he felt that it was fine for me to go home. He told me that he'd catch up with me over the weekend and fill me in "on the ongoing investigation." I hate cop talk!

I hung up with Joe, packed Lanny in my luggage compartment, fired up the scooter, and headed home.

As I drove down the Taconic, it sunk in that it had been only two days since Frankie was killed. It seemed like weeks, probably because so much had occurred in such a short time – a murder, intrigue, robbery, arrest, dislocation from my home – all in 48 hours. Wow! The thought of robbery brought into focus the fact that I had no equipment waiting for me in my apartment. The rest of my ride was spent in devising a plan to fill that void.

Chapter 13 -- A New Computer

When I got home, I unpacked the scooter, and began to put my apartment back in order. There were piles of paper every place from the ransacking of my desk and cabinets by my recent guests. The noticeable absence of my two computers on my worktable was more than a little depressing and reminded me that I had to do something about getting computers immediately.

I began the computer hunt by calling Stan Veit, the editor of Computer Shopper and explaining my plight. Stan listened to my tale of woe and said "I can have a DOS machine sent to you. You'll have to write a review of it but you can probably keep it as long as you want. It will probably be an AST or maybe I can get a Tandy. I'll get on it in the morning. As far as a Mac goes, I can't help you. Maybe you can shake one out of Apple or a local dealer." I gave Stan the shipping address and thanked him profusely.

I next called Ed Ramos, owner of Super Business Machines on Trinity Place in lower Manhattan, told him my story, and threw myself on his mercy asking for credit toward a new Mac. Not quite unexpectedly, Ed agreed to give me a brand new Mac II on credit. While this represented a real upgrade on the one that was stolen, it also put me in the hole for the next 24 months.

Satisfied with my results, I went out for a run, a lot less

uneventful one than the last one, came home, showered, read a bit more of Lanny and went to sleep.

Friday morning, I woke up early and called Matty to catch him before he made any plans for the car. I filled him in on the previous twenty-four hours and told him that I'd need the car to go down to Super Business to pick up the Mac. We decided to grab a cup of coffee at the Capitol after he said the nine o'clock Mass and, if he could get away, he would ride down with me to get the Mac.

When I was on my way out, I ran into John O'Rourke, the super. "Jackie, what was all that with the police here the other day?"

"Some fellows broke into my apartment but I was on my way home and saw them loading my computers into a car so I called the thirty-fourth. They got here in time to get one of the folks but the others got away with my stuff."

"Damn, that's too bad, Jackie. Did they get much?"

"They got my computers but that's about it. I have a new one coming by Fed Ex or UPS. It may get dropped at your apartment if I'm not home."

"Ok, I'll look for it."

I said "Thanks, John." and I was off.

I walked through the park, approaching where the whole

thing had begun. When I reached where Frankie's body had been, I saw the remnants of the police chalk line and what may have been a drop of blood where his head had lain. The whole thing gave me the willies all over again.

I walked down Isham Street and into the side door of Good Shepherd, coming in just as Matty arrived on the altar. When Mass ended, I went out the front door and walked down to the Capitol, saying hello to a number of locals as I walked. I find a comfort in knowing people and faces as I walk through my neighborhood, a comfort that I hadn't realized that I missed when I lived downtown. While I missed my children greatly, I realized that I would have gone onto becoming a very different person, a person that I would probably now consider someone vapid. I see more and more what the McMullens cherish in having greater control over their own lives.

I stopped at Benny's candy store for the papers – even though it was in its third ownership since Ben sold it, it was still Benny's – and went into the Capitol. I took the front booth, ordered coffee and English's for Matty and I. I was halfway through the Times editorials when Matty eased into the booth.

"Boy, you had some hell of a few days."

"Yeah, it wasn't as scary as it moved along but, once I could stop to think about it, it shook me a bit and having to replace the computers is a real pain in the ass."

"You wanted a new Mac anyhow."

"Not enough to go into debt for."

"So work harder – and offer it up."

My brother, the priest, had a great way of lifting my spirits!

As we rode downtown, Matty filled me in on the latest Paulist gossip. "There is a good chance that Kevin Devine will be assigned back here to Good Shepherd when he retires from the Army. I hope that the powers-that-be don't decide that one Devine is enough for Good Shepherd."

Kevin Devine, no relation to Matty or I, had grown up on 213th Street and spent his early years as a Paulist in Good Shepherd before becoming a Chaplain in the Army where he had won a Silver Star in Vietnam. To make matters more confusing, one of Kevin's brothers, an FBI agent, is named Matty.

"God, it doesn't seem like 25 years since he went in. I guess it could be confusing, calling the rectory and asking for Father Devine. It sounds like you've become attached to this place."

"I'll try not to be too attached in case I do have to move, but, yes, it's a real kick being a priest in your old neighborhood."

When we got to "Super Biz," Matty waited in the car. Most New York cops look the other way when it is a priest double parked and, while Matty was in his civilian clothes, we had a "Priest on Call" sign on the windshield. I went in the store, thanked Ed while signing my life away and carried the Mac out to the car.

While we just exchanged small talk on the way back uptown, I could tell that Matty was still concerned about my safety. I tried to assure him that the danger was over and told him that Joe was coming by tomorrow just to wrap everything up.

When we got to the house, Matty said that he should get back. "Russ Ryan's going out this afternoon and I should be around," so, after I got a cart from O'Rourke to take the Mac upstairs, Matty drove off. I took the Mac upstairs, brought the cart back, collected two days of mail, and went upstairs to set up my new computer.

Offering It Up

Chapter 14 -- My Couch Goes High Tech

I woke up early, excited at the prospect of putting together a new Macintosh -- the Mac II was the first expandable Macintosh. In 1985, Apple co-founder Steve Jobs had been forced out of Apple, in part, because he opposed "opening the Mac" to third party connectivity. Although I'd been a big fan of Jobs since the earliest days of Apple, I was against him in this one and, as I opened the cartons, I was almost happy that the older Macintosh had gone off the way it did. Once I had the computer up on the table and the cables, keyboard, and mouse next to it, I paused to put coffee on. I thought about taking the carton downstairs to the trash but decided that I better hang onto it for a few days in case, God forbid, there was something wrong with the computer and it had to go back.

As I finished the first cup and was about to start the second, the phone rang. It was Joe.

"Hi, I just got in from a run. As soon as I shower, I'll come up to you. I should be there about 9:30 or so. Ok? We have a bunch of things to go over."

That didn't sound good. "That's fine. I'm here setting up a computer."

"You got a new one? Good. I wouldn't put much hope in getting the old one back if I were you."

"That's what I thought and I couldn't wait. Ok. I'll see you when you get here."

"Right." And he was gone.

"A bunch of things to go over?" I had hoped that I was about out of it. The cops had the diskettes, Frankie's note, and the heavy who broke in here. I had been merely a conduit from Frankie to the cops or, rather, I wished that were the case. The threatening call, the ransacking of my apartment, the guy with the gun in my apartment, and the FBI lad telling me to "get out of Dodge" led me to believe that it were otherwise.

I returned to my Mac II and had it all set up and running by the time that Joe rang the bell.

I let him in. "Want coffee?"

"No, I stopped at the Perk and had a cup. I'm all ready to work. Finished with the computer?"

"For the time being. I have another machine, a DOS system arriving next week, I hope."

"Another computer? What do you need two for?"

I started to explain about different operating systems, file formats, graphical user interfaces and then stopped. Joe knew zero to nothing about computers, other than the fact that they might contain evidence, and he meant to keep it that way. "It's like two different religions -- Catholic and Jewish -- and

I consult to both and write about both, so I need both."

Joe nodded, "Which one is the Jew?"

The question threw me for a moment until I realized that he was joking.

I changed the subject before it got even wackier.

"Well, it's all set up. Want to see how a Macintosh works? It's quite different from the computers that most use."

"Most use? I don't use any computers, and, until I have to, I won't. I think, unfortunately, that I may have to at some point, unless I'm lucky enough to retire first."

"Ok, then. Let's gets started." I sat down at my kitchen table, waving Joe into a chair, and pulled a pad over to write on. "What's with the lots to go over?"

Joe took out a pad from the briefcase he was carrying, scanned it for a moment, and began, "The good news -- Tommy Napoli is rolling over on his cousin, Norris, and the whole deal. He knows that he can go for life so he's trying hard to cut a deal. He can tie his cousin to the Ford murder. He, of course, swears that he knew nothing until it had happened. He says that it was Serge Passarella, one of the slugs who was up here, that actually did the deed and that he didn't know about it until he heard Passarella telling Billy how well it went."

That was great. The guy who had killed Frankie had dropped in on me for a chat, the diskettes, and, probably, my life. "So how is Norris tied into the whole thing? And what ties Frankie to Napoli?"

"Norris was the money launderer, the investor. Our computer people say that the diskettes that you gave me show two sets of books for each company; the phony set and the real one. It was Napoli's money in at least one, if not all, of the companies. Ford was apparently the accountant who was supposed to make this all seem legal. From his note to you, he seemed not to have originally known what was going on. When he wised up, he tried to get out. Napoli couldn't let that happen – all we need to do is prove that it is his money being laundered and the Treasury guys can seize all his assets."

Joe paused for breath and went on, "We could probably have tied Napoli to the whole thing just through the information on the diskettes but now the cousin locks it up. He's told us that Norris came to Napoli, worried about Ford and being there when Passarella reported killing Ford. He also was in this place at Napoli's direction expressly trying to recover the computer evidence. His testimony ties Ford, Norris, and Napoli into one tight little ball."

"Sounds like a slam dunk to me."

"It is – if the slug makes it to trial."

"What? Can't you protect him?"

"We can 90 to 95% guarantee it – but you're never 100% sure. All we need is one leak. – and, worse, if there is any Russian Mafia money involved, those scumbags will attack like an army if they can find where to go."

Joe was making me very nervous. "Great – and how am I involved in all of this?"

"Not as much as you would have been if we didn't have Tommy – but you and this apartment are still the direct link from Frankie to Napoli. Frankie was sending you evidence against Norris and, it seems, Napoli. So Napoli had him killed and had this place burglarized. You're at the hub of that."

I thought about that for a second. "So, do I need any protection? And my kids will be here for most of the summer. What are the chances of someone coming back looking for what Tommy's buddies missed?"

"I'd say zero to none. All the players know that we have at least Tommy and probably all the evidence. I'd say that the only person in real danger now is Norris. We're trying to roll him but he's holding out. If Napoli or the Russians think that he is the only link to them, he's gone."

It must have been obvious that I wasn't convinced so Joe said "But we're not leaving you out in the cold. We'll keep the tap on your phone – don't worry about personal things – as soon as we hear that it's a personal call, we cut out." Yeah, sure!

Joe went on "and I've got some folks coming over in within the hour to set up another gizmo. Can you go take another ride or something for a few hours?" I reluctantly agreed to leave and took the scooter up to New Rochelle, rode around Iona, went over to the Sound and read for a while in the park, and then stopped back by Iona for a hamburger in the Beechmont before heading home.

When I got back upstairs about 4:30, Joe was still there and was grinning, "We operated on your couch."

"What? On my couch?"

"Don't worry. You can't see a thing and we have the neatest thing installed in it. This was developed by the CIA in the 70s. We just got out hands on it. We modified it a little. Your couch is now plugged into an outlet so we don't have to worry about batteries, and it will just work automatically. When you sit down on the left side as you face it and lean on the armrest, it will automatically kick off a recording device and anything said in the room will be picked up. Once the device is activated, if you think that you're in immediate danger, kicking the couch leg with your right foot will have someone here immediately. When you stand up, it will transmit for another two minutes and then close down. We'll keep this in place right up through the trial. Feel any better?"

I nodded and then remembered the kids. "What am I going to do during the summer when John and Becky are here? How do I keep them off the couch?"

"Put a sheet over it. Tell them it's broken and you're waiting for the re-upholstery. Make up some additional bull shit to make it work."

I was dubious but thought there was a chance that it could fly.

We talked a little while longer, moving off into neighborhood topics, and then Joe said, "I should be going. I have to stop by the office for a bit and I'm supposed to meet some guys from the Prep tonight – Richie Scarlata, Joe Martin, Tommy Kelly, and a few others. John Donnelly's passing through town and we're getting together." Donnelly was an Air Force officer who had gone to the now defunct Manhattan Prep and Manhattan College with the rest.

"Give them my regards. I know them all but Martin. Scarlata lived across the street and Donnelly lived next door to McMullen."

"You probably met Martin at McMullen's after the race a few years ago. He lives up there. He's married to Joanne Campbell." John had organized a long-distance relay team for a "Manhattan-to-Mahopac" race. Joe was one of the runners; the rest were Artie Burns, Frank Mulderrig, Gene Schneider, Bill McLoughlin, Jim Connors, Denis O'Sullivan, and Willie Kay. They ran the 36 miles under the name "Good Shepherd Boys Club" and the best thing to say about the effort was that they finished. The race was followed by a party at the Lake at John's house for about 150 of our immediate friends. Bob Cummings, Bobby Sturgis, and

Timmy Luddy came up from Houston, and others came from all over. It was a memorable party.

"I'm sure I did, but wouldn't know him now if I fell over him, but I remember Joanne. I would have asked her out years ago if Mike Ryan didn't beat me to it."

Joe laughed, "She's better off. I introduced her to Joe after she and Mike stopped going out."

On that note, we said our goodbyes and Joe was off.

Chapter 15 -- A Quiet Summer

The summer, and the children, came and went. It was pleasant and generally uneventful. We went camping for a week, went to Jones Beach, Tibbit's Brook, and the McMullens on day trips and, generally, the kids hung out in Inwood Park as I did growing up. John got into basketball games at the courts and, by mid-July, was accepted as a regular, while Becky, at twelve, was able to find a group of girls who hung around the same courts and, seemingly, picked up some male admirers; the phone rang often as the summer went on and, I imagined that the FBI was getting tired of listening to teenage girl-talk.

I also spent some time jogging, often with Frankie Almonte who had done very well on those Regents and was now off to Brown on a scholarship – actually he had the scholarship well before the exams but still had to do well to cement it. He was grateful that I had kept him away from the investigation as that might have jeopardized the scholarship. I saw why the Moose was proud of him and realized that I would miss him when he went off to Rhode Island.

Since the kids had the run of the park to themselves, I was able to do enough work to keep the cash flowing. My DOS computer, an AST, had arrived from Stan and, between it and my spanking new Mac, I was able to keep both the consulting work and the writing going. By the time that the progeny were due to return to their mother, we had fallen into such a comfortable routine that it was difficult to break it off. Additionally, it seemed that Becky was breaking some hearts as she went between smiles and tears as August 20th, their departure date approached. Finally, they were gone, off on a short vacation with their mother and stepfather before school began.

Feeling somewhat at loose ends after their departure, I spent a lot of time on the motor scooter and, more often than not, wound up at Guinan's. I had told the McMullens about Guinan's and, often, John and Barbara or just John would ride over to meet me or just happen to be there when I got there. John's children had also gone off on vacation with his first wife so we had a bit of shared loneliness. I also got to know Jim's wife Peg and two of his children, John and Margaret. It turned out that Margaret was a police officer in the McMullens' town, Yorktown.

Finally, as September rolled around, I put my nose to the grindstone. I was going to teach a course at the New School beginning the end of September and, between that preparation and my normal work, I had little time for scootering or other frivolities. Sometimes, if Matty were saying the noon Mass, I would drop in and, after Mass, go for a walk around the park with him.

One day, when it turned out that he couldn't go, I stopped into Minogue's and had a few beers while talking to Joe Gavin, who was "behind the stick." Joe had been a legendary drinker in his twenties and thirties but, when it started to get the best of him, Joe had stopped and, now, was a non-drinking bartender serving the neighborhood drink of choice to fools such as I (Although I had cut way back on drinking because of the business, I was thinking of stopping altogether as the McMullens had – but had not yet crossed the bridge.).

I spent a few hours, catching up on the neighborhood gossip and watching a Met game on the television. When the game ended, I bid adieu to Joe and walked slowly home, past my grammar school, into the park, past where Frank had died, past the playground, and into the house, all the time feeling lonely for the kids and lonely for the jump-shooting, hard-drinking hell-raiser that I once was.

Offering It Up

Chapter 16 -- Eileen Kilroy

On September 7th, the Sunday of the Labor Day weekend, I got crossed up with Matty. I was sure that he had told me that he was saying the 11:30 Mass in the main church but, when I stood for the beginning of Mass, it was Father Curtin who came though the sanctuary doors. Father Curtin was a very nice man and seemed to inspire some young folks but he always put me to sleep.

In the early days of my marriage to Margo, I had gotten away from going to church, Margo was not devout in any way and Sunday morning always seemed more conducive to sex than church – although I said God's name many times most Sunday mornings. After the children were born and baptized, I returned to regular attendance, taking one or both with me and, at times, accompanied by Margo. When the marriage began to go sour, Margo stopped all church participation as well as our communal orgasmic prayer.

After the split, my attendance fell off again, particularly if I were lucky enough to have a bedmate on a Sunday morning, but when I moved back to Inwood, first my mother and then Matty led me back to the church of my youth. The majesty of the liturgy gave me a peaceful comfort that I rarely felt outside of the church's walls—although Father Curtin had almost put me to sleep on this particular day.

I came down the long steps of Good Shepherd trying to decide whether I'd go up to the rectory to hunt up Matty or stop at the Capitol for a cup of coffee or just get the papers and head on home.

As I hit the street and looked around for a familiar face, I heard a soft voice behind me, "Hello, Jackie."

I turned and almost gasped. It was Eileen Kilroy, the love of my youth – probably of my life. "Eileen. How long has it been?"

"It's been just about sixteen years, Jackie. How are you?"

"Right now, Eileen, better than I have been in a long time, just seeing you."

"You still have a line, Jackie. Buy me a cup of coffee and we'll catch up."

Catch up? We had little to really catch up about. We had gone together all through high school and until just before my senior year at Iona. Eileen was going to be a junior at Marymount. I probably walked Eileen home from every

Friday Night Dance at Good Shepherd that I ever went to. We had been planning marriage for years with what seemed like deep love and commitment and then, in one weekend, it was all over and we really didn't speak again until now.

Eileen had been about to do a year in France while I did my accounting internship, getting ready to earn a year's salary that would have us ready for marriage as soon as she graduated. It all sounded great but, during the summer, it began to unravel as sex and Vietnam came together to have me figuratively climbing a wall. We had plenty of passion and petting but that was as far as it went. Fifteen years of Catholic education with visions of Hell and "offending God" had taken their hold on us. We were willing to stretch the line with petting and dry humping until orgasm but we knew that actual intercourse was crossing the line in a way that could not be undone.

But, in that summer, the pressures were greater than I could handle.

"Goddamn it, Eileen, you'll be gone for a fucking year."

"Jackie, you know I don't like you to say that – and it is only 9 months."

"And I could be drafted as soon as you get home."

"It's still a mortal sin, Jackie, no matter what happens."

"We love each other, Eileen."

"All the more reason to wait, Jackie."

... and so it went, usually ending with me sighing, taking her into my arms and kissing her with my hands all over her until the grinding brought us both to orgasm and, for the moment, the stress was gone. At least that was the pattern until the first Friday in August. We had planned an early night. Eileen had to be down at Marymount early on Saturday morning to meet with her advisors and the other students that would be going abroad to go over what they had to bring with them, to ensure that their passports were in order, and, in general, get ready to go. We had a soda in Broger's and I walked her home about 8:00. We detoured into the park and were sitting on steps in a deserted area, kissing and feeling until I felt that I was going to burst. I guided her hand down to my cock. She had squeezed it through my clothes on occasion before but, this time, even that was not enough. I slid my hand down, moved her hand, opened my zipper, and tried to guide her hand inside.

She froze, almost recoiling from me. "Jackie, what are you doing?"

My hardon collapsed. "What do you think I'm doing, Eileen? I can't take this anymore."

"Then don't take it anymore. Good night, Jackie." She was on her feet, straightening her clothes and gone!

I got up slowly, zipped up, and started walking home, feeling too low to head down to the Broadstone where I knew my friends would be. I cut around the baseball field to the entrance to the park and, as I turned, almost bowled over Rita Schwartz.

"Whoa, Jackie. Sleepwalking?"

"No, Rita, just miserable."

Rita had been a close friend for years, although most of our friends, Eileen included, didn't know of the relationship. I was Irish Catholic and Rita "was of the Jewish persuasion," and, while we had a few Jewish guys hanging out with us, ones who liked to drink and play cards, there was usually a social line that wasn't crossed. Rita had let me know very early in the game that her parents would never approve of me taking her out; they barely tolerated us talking on the phone. She explained that "we were both English majors" and we were discussing academic things, and, since, for most of the last three years, she was safely ensconced at Brandeis in

Boston, they grudgingly accepted the phone calls. They never knew that I was really an Accounting major. Some nights, after the park was fairly empty, we sat in the playground on benches, talking, telling each other everything that was on our minds, knowing that, were the religions not a problem, it might have been Rita and Jackie, rather than Eileen and Jackie – or not, because we may not have been as open. I knew when Rita gave up her virginity and she knew that I, unfortunately, still had mine. We talked about religion, politics, books, anything; we respected each other's intelligence and opinions.

So, it was only natural that I poured everything out to Rita – the sexual frustration, the impending separation, the fear of the draft, everything. By the time I was finished, we were standing by the 214th Street playground, it was almost dark and starting to get a little chilly.

"Jackie. My parents are away and I have some meatballs and spaghetti upstairs. Why don't you go down to Murray's and get some beer and soda – get me cherry or root beer – and some ice cream for desert. I'll go heat up the food?" I had rarely been to Rita's floor, never mind in her apartment and she had never been in mine, even though we lived right across the street from each other.

"Murray's may be closed; I'll have to go over to Ryan's, but sure."

"Ok. Do that."

As I walked over to Ryan's on 218th near Broadway, I hoped that one of my closest friends, Mike Ryan, wasn't working in his father's store. The last thing I wanted to mention was my tiff with Eileen or where I was going with the beer, soda, and ice cream but, as luck would have it, young Joey Donnelly was working and I was heading back to Rita's within a few minutes.

I rang Rita's bell and, before she buzzed me in, she said through the speaker "The door's open. Lock it after you and put the stuff in the refrigerator. I'll be out in a minute."

I did as I was told and, when I went into the living room, I heard her voice from behind a door, "Come in here."

I pushed the door open and I was in her bedroom with her in an open robe, naked under it, standing in front of me. She moved to me and put her arms around my neck, rubbing her breasts against my tee shirt. She brought her lips to mine and, as we kissed with our tongues touching, my whole body came alive. She grinded into me as I explored her mouth, her hand sliding to my ass and pulling me in tighter caressing my hardon with her body.

She broke the kiss and sat on the edge of the bed, her hands going to my belt and opening it. I looked down at her and my breath came faster. She pushed my jeans and boxers down. "Kick them off, Jackie." As I kicked off my shoes and stepped out of the pants, she stroked my very hard cock and licked at the head. "ohhhhhh … yes."

She took it in her mouth and sucked it ... in and out. I had never had such a feeling, "Rita .. ummmm .. God .. yes."

She lay back on the bed and guided me, by my wet hard cock, up onto the bed. She spread her legs and guided me up into her. "Now fuck me, Jackie." and I did.

I had never had such a feeling ... of passion ... of joy … of joining ... it seemed as though it lasted forever ... but was over too soon. "Ohhh ... fuck ... Rita ... God ... fuck" until I finally exploded into her and collapsed onto her. "My God, that was wonderful."

"Yes, it was, Jackie -- and this is just the beginning."

"Hmmmm … how late will your parents be out?"

"Until Sunday evening. How late can you stay?"

"Until Sunday afternoon, if you'll have me that long."

"I'll have had you over and over by then."

"Let me use your phone."

I called home and was lucky enough to get Matty, home from the Seminary.

"Matty, I just met Buzz Sweeney in the Broadstone and he's off to Rockaway for the weekend. I'm going to go out with him. We can probably stay in Chickie's aunt's bungalow. Tell Mom I'll call her tomorrow. They're out in front with the car. I gotta go."

And that was that. Rita and I spent the whole weekend together. With her as the teacher, I learned so much, not only about the physical aspects of sex but about the join, fun, and love. We not only had oral sex, she taught just where to lick and nibble – I learned to put my fingers in her and tease her ... we masturbated for each other ... we tried every position we could think of -- me on top, on the bottom, behind her. We showered together and with the water splashing on her back, she sucked my cock.

Along the way, I broke with my Church on the whole concept of sex as sinful. Our lovemaking – and, no mater what Rita and I did, it was lovemaking – was joyous and spiritual as well as physical. God had given us our bodies to use and enjoy. As long as we were honest with each other, and Rita and I were honest with each other, I could never see anything that weekend as the slightest bit sinful.

When it dawned on me that I might be making her pregnant and changing our lives, she assured me that she was using a diaphragm. She showed me how she put it in , and then we fucked immediately.

As we held each other, all fucked out for a while, I said "That was wonderful."

"You have no idea how wonderful. It was very special. I've been with three men. You're the fourth and this was very different. The first was just to get rid of this virginity and it was not really pleasant and a little painful. The second was with a boy friend who I had a continuing relationship, but it was always either to go along with him or to please me. It never seemed to be about an "us." I didn't realize it until just now, we were joining, giving and taking at the same time. It was beautiful."

"I agree – and what about the other guy?"

"Oh. That was after I broke up with Seth. I was down and just wanted to get laid. I let some guy pick me up and take me home and have at me. It was dumb. I won't do that again, or at least I hope, I won't."

"I hope you won't too."

"Hmmm … you left love marks on my breasts. It's a good thing my mother won't see them. She'd go ballistic or maybe she wouldn't if she thought they were put there by a Jewish doctor."

I laughed and pushed her head down toward my cock again. "Here ... put some love marks here." and she did.

Eventually, I said "What happens now? I don't want to be a one-night ... actually a two-night stand."

"Jackie, we'll always be special for each other and, when we can, we'll get together, I promise, but you know that I'll marry some Jewish professional and you'll probably be back with Eileen. All we can say is that this is special and we are special." We were special and, for years, even when we were married to others, we got together when we could, not often, but enough to always re-kindle that weekend. It was never quite as memorable as the first weekend but always better than with any other woman. I seemed connected deeper with

Rita than with any other woman in my life with the possible exception of Eileen.

When I finally did leave Rita's, I walked down to Broadway to get cigarettes and, as I was walking back up 207th Street, ran into Eileen. "You went to Rockaway? We parted like that and you went to Rockaway and left me miserable here?"

"We didn't part; you ran off ... and I really didn't go to Rockaway."

"Where were you then?"

"I was with an old friend ... a woman."

She looked at me unbelieving and I felt awful for being about to hurt her ... but I didn't feel guilty.

"A woman? I know all your friends -- who? – and what happened?"

I didn't say anything, just shook my head.

"Did you have sex?"

"Yes, I did."

"You fucked another woman???" and she slapped me hard across the face, turned and ran up the block.

They were the last words that Eileen Kilroy had spoken to me until she wanted to "catch up." I knew that she had gone to France and returned and graduated from Marymount. I knew that she had married a fellow from Manhattan College named Maher and had a few children after moving to Rockland County. I almost called her when I heard that her husband had been killed in an auto accident, but I was still trying to make my marriage with Margo work and thought better of it.

Offering It Up

Chapter 17 -- We Catch Up

We stopped at the Golden Rule rather than walking the extra block to the Capitol and, once we were settled and had ordered coffees and English muffins, Eileen went right into her story. "You know I got married almost right out of college, Jackie. My roommate when I was in France was Rosemary Maher from Rye and, while we were over there, her family came to visit. I met her brother Jim then and he asked if he could write to me. We got close by mail and, when I came back, we starting dating. He was already two years out of Manhattan and working so we got married as soon as I got out of school."

I listened quietly, nodding from time-to-time, thinking that the scenario was almost the exact one that we had planned.

"We had two children fairly quickly, great boys, Jim Jr. and Tommy, and bought a house in Nanuet after little Jimmy was born. All was wonderful until some drunk on the Palisades Interstate Parkway, going the wrong way killed Jim one Friday night about 2AM when he was coming home late from work."

"God, I'm sorry, Eileen."

"It was over seven years ago. I've come to terms with it as well as I could and have tried to move on. Thank God, Jim had great insurance and I was financially okay and, then, Jim's partner from work, an old school friend took me under his wing and gave me a work-from-home job so I've done well."

"That's good. You've certainly dealt with a lot."

"And what about you, Jackie?"

By the time I had recounted my marriage, divorce, and move back to the neighborhood, we had finished a second round of English muffins and a few cups of coffee.

"So what brings you back to the neighborhood, Eileen?"

"You may remember my Aunt Ann, my mother's sister. She lived in our house, always kind of a recluse. She's not in good health so I've been coming back to look in on her from time to time. Jackie, want to take me for a walk around the park? I haven't done that in years."

I paid the bill and we cut through the alley by the church up to Copper Street, walked over past Seaman Avenue and into the Park. We walked slowly around the baseball fields, a walk that we had taken many times holding hands. When we reached Indian Road, Eileen stopped and looked across the street and said softly "Jackie, take me up to your apartment."

Without another word, we crossed the street, went in through the basement, took the elevator to six, and went down the hall into the apartment. We no sooner were through the door than she was in my arms and we were kissing with even more abandon than in our youth. I guided her right into my bedroom and we were out of our clothes in minutes. As I was pushing into her --- she fit me like a glove -- she said, "I never got over you, Jackie."

As I exploded into her, the whole sixteen years of our separation seemed to evaporate. "God, Eileen, I love you" just flew out of my lips and then I realized that I meant it. She whimpered "I love you too, Jackie" and began to cry.

I held her close "What's wrong? That was wonderful."

"I was so stupid, so fucking stupid to let you get away. We could have been together like this for years. Jim was a good husband, and the kids are wonderful, but he wasn't you, and I think he knew that you were always still the man in my life. If I could only do it over, you would be doing whatever you wanted to – put it in my cunt ... my mouth ... my ass ... whatever it took to please you."

I had never heard Eileen talk like that. It was both a shock and a turn-on. I grinned and said, "well, we always have now."

She took the hint and moved down my body, looking up as she began to lick me hard. "I'll expect the same from you." I, of course, complied as soon as she finished.

By the time we were worn out, it was dark out and Eileen said "I have to leave. I'll go see my aunt and then take off for home. Do you have the same number? I'll call you the next time I am coming in."

"I sure do – and what's yours?"

She looked at me "You can't call me. I live with Jim's old partner. Remember, I mentioned him before. He was very good to me, Jackie, after Jim died and I came to lean on him, perhaps too much. I'm very grateful to him, but I want much more of you."

She paused and then said, more quietly. "Can you accept me on those terms?"

It took me less than thirty seconds to take her back into my arms and whisper, "Yes, Eileen. I can and I will," and, then laughing, we took time for one more "quickee."

Chapter 18 -- Get Out Of Town Again

We went on like this for almost three months, getting together once or twice a week, rarely leaving the apartment. I wanted to take her out for a meal or walks but she was concerned that her aunt, who already thought less of her because she was living with a guy not her husband, would hear about us through the grapevine that was Inwood. She even made me swear that I would keep Matty in the dark.

One day in late October, when I had run out to get some food at Murray's before she arrived, I met her parking her car as I left Murray's. As we walked along, I looked across Indian Road and saw Eddie Winne out in the park. Eddie, a Merchant Seaman, got home to the neighborhood rarely and, I said "There's Eddie Winne. Let's stop and say hello." Eileen only walked faster. "I told you, Jackie, that I only want to see you. I don't want it getting back to my aunt or to Bill. Do you think Eddie saw us?" Even though I wasn't sure if he had seen us, I said "No," knowing that he was probably shipping out soon anyhow.

So, we worked hard at keeping the new "us" to ourselves and it was one of the few things that I hadn't shared with Matty.

Margo dropped the kids off for Thanksgiving so I missed almost a full week of Eileen, but she said that she had to spend some time with Bill and her kids anyhow. The week gave me time to think, though. The newness of the sex was starting to wear off and, although it was still wonderful, I knew that I wanted more from Eileen. I wanted for her to make a commitment to us; to break off from Bill and to start a life with just us. I knew that it was probably unreasonable to push for this until after the Christmas holidays but I knew it was what I wanted.

I missed Eileen like crazy and was disappointed when she called on Monday and said that she couldn't make it until Friday morning. She had things to do around her home, but that we could spend most of the day on Friday, a one-day honeymoon.

I spent Wednesday working on a database design for a manufacturing client, paid some bills, and then, around 6 PM, walked in the snow down to Broadway for a hamburger in McSherry's. When I walked in, I saw Eddie Winne at the bar talking with John Higgins; I waved and grabbed a booth to order and read a little. Matty had gotten me into Thomas Merton; I had thought of him only as the monk and writer of the rather syrupy "Seven Storey Mountain" but Matty had pointed out that Dan Berrigan, the anti-war Jesuit who I admired had regarded Merton as a mentor and, half-way through 'Raids on the Unspeakable," I could understand why.

I was halfway through my hamburger and Merton's essay on Flannary O'Connor when Eddie appeared at the table.

"Ed, I was going to come over when I finished the hamburger."

"I have to run. I'm shipping out again tomorrow and I have to be up early. Was that Eileen Kilroy I saw you with a few months ago?"

"Yes. I ran into her a while back after Mass one Sunday."

"Gee, I haven't seen her since her aunt died – and I hadn't seen her for years before that."

"Her aunt – the one on 207th Street?"

"Yeah. It must have been four or five years ago, before you moved back. I just happened to see her. I was passing the church when the funeral ended. I got to talk to her for a few minutes. She said that her aunt was so close to Eileen's mother that they had thought that she wouldn't last long after Mrs. Kilroy died and she didn't -- less than a year. I had been at sea when Mrs. Kilroy died. Why is something the matter?"

"No. I just didn't know that they had died so close. My mother called me when Mrs. Kilroy died. She went to the funeral."

I wanted to change this subject fast. "Where are you off to?"

"The Med – then South America. It should be good weather but I'll be away for the holidays. I won't be back until the end of January."

"Well, I hope you have a good time in the ports."

"I always do, or, at least, try to. Hey, I better take off. I still have packing to do."

"Let me pay the check and make a quick call over on the pay phone and I'll walk up with you."

"Ok. I'll say goodbye to the guys at the bar. Give me a sign when you're ready."

I paid the check and left the tip and then looked up Joe's home number and called him.

After exchanging sarcastic pleasantries, I told him where I was and asked him if he could do a quick check on Eileen Kilroy Maher.

"Your old girlfriend, Eileen Kilroy? The FBI's not in the lonely hearts business, fellow."

When I filled him in briefly, finishing with my conversation with Eddie, he relented and told me to call him around ten in the morning. "I'll get in early and get it out of the way."

I waved to Eddie and we walked up Broadway to 218^{tth} Street and then the block to Eddie's. Along the way, we reminisced about some of our crazy acts over the years and, when we reached his house, he said "Hey, I have a refrigerator full of beer. Why don't you come up and have a few? I can pack while we talk."

It didn't take much to sell me. I knew that I wouldn't sleep much at home with the confusion about Eileen running around in my head. "Sure. Sounds great."

Well, a few turned into more than a few and I wound up sleeping at Ed's.

In the morning, I helped Ed carry his stuff down to the corner and hail a cab. I had a real hunger, and instead of going home, I jumped in the cab with Ed and told the cabbie to drop me at Isham Street by the Church.

"I'll do the 9 o'clock Mass if Mattie's saying it and then hit the Capitol."

"Give my regards to Matty. He's a good guy."

"He is that."

I said goodbye to Ed again, got out of the cab, and climbed the long steps to Good Shepherd. Matty wasn't saying the Mass; Father Russ Ryan was, so I stayed anyhow. Maybe God would reveal what was going on.

He didn't.

I walked down to the Capitol, had juice, coffee and an English and, at 10 on the dot, was around the corner in the phone booth in Benny's calling Joe.

When he came on the phone, he sounded agitated. "Jesus. Where the hell have you been?"

"Where have I been? You said 10 o'clock. I called exactly at ten."

"I know. I know. I've been trying to reach you since 8. There's been some developments."

"Developments?"

"Yeah. Tommy Napoli was stabbed to death in Riker's last night."

"Wow. Who did it? Why?"

"Nobody's been charged yet but, more importantly, you're now the main witness that ties Ford, Norris, and Napoli together and, when I couldn't get you at home. I was worried. I called Jim Finn at the 34th and asked him to send a car up to check on you. Hold on. I better call him on the other line and have him call it off."

While I waited, my mind was running amok. "Holy shit. If Napoli had his cousin killed and I was the only one still in his way … son of a bitch."

My reverie was interrupted. "I'm back. I guess you see the problem."

"Yup. It sounds like I'm both a target and bait."

"That you are, and there's more," and then he told me about Eileen.

When he finished, I was silent. Then he said, "When are you supposed to see her next?"

"She's coming over tomorrow morning."

"Great, so we have to keep you alive at least until then. Where can you go and bury yourself until tomorrow morning?"

"Hmm. I could go up to John and Barbara's. You know where they are." Joe had run in the Manhattan-to-Mahopac relay race and had been to their house then and other times as well.

"That's a great place to go. Do you know any local cops up there?"

"No, why would I … wait a minute. Jim Guinan's daughter, Margaret, is on the Yorktown force."

"That's Margaret Guinan? G U I N A N?"

"Yes."

"I'll call her and ask her to swing by. What's the actual address there?"

"I don't think they have one. It's the boonies. They don't even have mail delivery. When I UPS them things. I have to write on the package "Big Red Barn, Fourth Driveway on the Right going up the hill on Perry Street, Jefferson Valley, NY 10535.""

"Slow down. That's the fourth driveway? ... and Terry Street? T E R R Y?"

"No, Perry with P ... and it is the fourth driveway."

"Ok. I'll give her a call. Now, can you be back in your apartment at nine tomorrow, no earlier and not much later? I'll have the place covered today and tonight."

"Ok. I can do that."

"Good. I'll go up to your apartment. I think I still have the key you gave me. If not, does the super have a key?"

"Yes. His name is O'Rourke."

"Good. That's taken care of. Now, if you want to talk to me, call your number, let it ring twice, hang up, and call back. I'll only answer calls that come in like that. You have an answering machine, right?"

"Yes."

"So you won't miss any messages. What's McMullen's number?"

I gave him John's number and then he gave me some more instructions and then hung up.

I dialed the number I had just given Joe.

"John McMullen."

"Hi. It's Jackie. Got a room I can stay in tonight?"

"Sure. The kids aren't here. We have plenty of room. Got a problem?'

I summarized what was going on and mentioned that I'd stop in the mall near his house and get some clothes.

"Great, I'll tell Barbara. Give me a call when you get to the mall. We'll come over and have lunch in the Food Court – pizza or a sandwich."

"Sounds like a plan. I'll talk to you soon."

"See ya."

Then I called the Good Shepherd Rectory to tell Matty that I had to take the car. The receptionist told me that he was over at the school talking to the 8th grade so I left a message with her and asked her to have the school maintenance man unlock the chain fence so I could get the car out.

Then I walked up to the school yard, took the car, and went off to Jefferson Valley, NY.

Offering It Up

Chapter 19 -- Jefferson Valley

I took my time, very unlike my normal driving, trying to the best of my ability to ensure that there was no one behind me – the last thing that I wanted to do was to bring my safety problems to the McMullens. It was bad enough that I was just barging in on them. I turned right out of the convent parking lot, turned left on Broadway, went north over the Broadway Bridge, turned right onto 230th Street and then went south on the Major Deegan Expressway, all the time looking in the rearview mirror. Almost satisfied that no one was following me, I got off at the next exit, Fordham Road, turned left and got right back on the Deegan, heading north. I passed the exit I had originally gotten on, heading the opposite direction, and went one more to the Van Courtland Park South exit, turning right off the exit to Broadway and then right again, up Broadway to the northbound entrance for the Saw Mill River Parkway.

By this time, I had probably wasted an hour but I had some degree of certainty that I was not bringing trouble north with me. I turned on WFUV-FM and settled in for the thirty-five mile trip north, a drive up the Saw Mill to the Taconic State Parkway and then north on the Taconic to the Jefferson Valley Route 6 Exit.

As I drove, I tried to make sense of the events of the last six months; they had been a roller coaster – Frank's murder, the robbery, the apprehension, the finding of Guinan's, work, summer with the kids, Eileen, another murder, and, now, fleeing again; shock, fear, friendship, peace, joy, sex, shock, and anger. I finally gave up trying to make sense of it, listened to the radio and thought of what I needed at the mall and what I might get there for Barbara as a token in thanks for the hospitality.

As I went north on the Taconic, I was, as always, captivated by the natural beauty so close to New York City. By the time I passed over the Croton Dam Bridge on the Taconic, I felt a lot better than at any time since running into Eddie in McSherry's. Shortly, I passed Mohansic State Park and four exits later was off the Taconic, turning right onto Route 6, and then into the mall parking lot.

I shopped for a while, picking up some clothes – jeans, shirt, underwear, sox, and even pajamas and a robe – at Sears. I found a gold frog pin at Zales's Jewelry for Barbara and then stopped in Waldenbooks to browse. It only took me fifteen minutes to pick up the new Max Allen Collins' Nate Heller mystery, The "God Game," a science fiction mystery by Andrew Greeley, and a biography of Dorothy Day by William Miller. I cannot pass a bookstore without going in and, once inside, find it very difficult to leave without buying something. I had long mused that this affliction must have something to do with the water in Inwood as it is shared by John, his older brother Bud, Mike Ryan, and Matty.

I called John from the payphone by the front door, stored my purchases in the car, and returned to meet Barbara and him in front of Brannigan's, a restaurant just inside the Mall entrance. We had decided on the phone that lunch there would be somewhat more relaxed than at the food court upstairs.

As we were being seated by the hostess, John said "Hey, there's Joe and Maureen McKenna. You know Joe – and Maureen, Jackie Walsh' sister." "Very well", I replied, and we walked over to their table to say hello as Barbara secured our table.

"Joe … Maureen" They looked up, did a double take and smiled. As we shook hands with Joe and kissed Maureen, Barbara joined us and told me that "Luke played baseball in a league with Joe and Maureen's son." John added "Vinnie Bernadetto had a son in the league too."

We chatted for a while as I dwelt on the joys of motor scootering and I said to Joe "You should be taking one back and forth to the 34th. It would be a great ride." Joe smiled and said "Maybe I should," but, from the look on Maureen's face, it would be a cold day in hell before that happened.

As we turned to leave, Joe said "Nice to see you" and then, looking at me, "Maybe I'll see you tomorrow." I just said "Ok" as the exchange brought me back to why I was here and not in Inwood.

Over lunch I recounted the events of the last few months, including my involvement with Eileen. Barbara had come into John's life long after my split with Eileen and had never met her so she had a number of questions about her. Neither of them were blatant enough to ask "Well, have you been fucking her?" but you could tell they assumed that I had.

Lunch continued through a lot of coffee and, by the time we were finished, I had answered every question that they had. John said "Enough, let's go home and get you settled." Over my objections, he grabbed the check, saying "You might get killed tomorrow and then I'd owe you and wouldn't be able to pay you back." Barbara scowled "What an awful thing to say" and walked toward the door. We followed her and drove to their house – they had their scooters and I had the car.

Once back at their house, a 220-year-old barn that they have been modifying since they moved in, the rest of the day went fairly rapidly and was very enjoyable. John had set up a dinner with a small number of local friends that I knew from parties at his house. I was able to get a short nap, shower, and put on some of the new clothes that I had bought before leaving for an eight o'clock at a favorite restaurant of theirs, Yogi's Dutch Barn. We were a few minutes late and turned out to be the last ones arriving. The Caseys had just, we were told, preceded us and the Katzs and Friedmans had been there a few minutes.

The Yogi's food was terrific. I had a favorite of mine, a fried fillet of flounder, and the portion was enormous. More importantly, the company was great. Jim Casey was an old neighborhood friend and had grown up in the house that I live in. His wife, Barbara, an ex-Peace Corps volunteer, was delightful company. The Katzs, both named Barry (Barrie for her), which regularly confused people, were animated and interesting and the Friedmans, Ron and Doris, had been friends for a good while. Ron was the McMullens' dentist and had recently become mine.

The evening went rapidly and, with good conversation and good food, I had almost forgotten my situation as a possible target.

When we got back to McMullens', I called home, let it ring twice, hung up, and called back. Joe picked up immediately. He didn't waste any time with pleasantries.

"Eileen left a message on the machine. She says she'll be here about ten. You better be back here about eight thirty."

"Ok."

"Call me from one of those gas stations on 230th Street – same two rings and hang up. Then I'll know how close you are. Park on Indian Road and come in through the basement. If you recognize any of our people on the street, just pass them by and keep walking. I'll be in the basement. Got it?"

"Yes."

"Ok see you then. I don't want anyone calling this number and getting a busy signal. Bye." and he was gone.

I reprised the conversation for the McMullens. Barbara said, "He sounds concerned. You better be careful."

John said "It sounds like a very thorough plan to me. You'll be alright."

I think I came down on Barbara's side.

I went to bed soon after and, surprisingly, slept like a baby.

Chapter 20 -- The Shoe Drops

The alarm woke me at six-thirty. I had been in the midst of a rather confusing dream in which both Eileen and Rita had a part – some things never change. I was up, showered, and ready to go by seven. I turned down Barbara's offer of breakfast, saying "I'll grab coffee at the deli at the bottom of the hill" and, after they both admonished me to be careful and to call them, I was out the door and in the car.

The ride down the Taconic and the Saw Mill was uneventful, giving me time to dwell on my relationship with Eileen and what I had gotten myself into since I chased Franklin Almonte through the park. I got off the parkway at 239th Street, came down Riverdale Avenue, and stopped on 230th Street at Kingsdale Exxon to fill up and to call Joe. When I got through to him and told him that I was about five minutes away, he reviewed my parking plan, telling me, "Don't worry about alternate parking today. You won't get a ticket." The fact that all law enforcement agencies in New York seemed to be on the case made me feel somewhat better.

I followed Broadway across the bridge to Manhattan Island, turned right on 218th Street, and, at its end, turned left on Indian Road. As I drove slowly up the block looking for a parking space, I saw Kevin Reilly sitting on a park bench reading the Daily News and, as I moved a little further up the block, I passed a car with Joe McKenna sitting in the driver's seat. I found a legal spot just before the corner, parked the car, and crossed the street to my building. The game was on!

Joe was in the basement as I came in and, acting as though he didn't know me, he pressed the elevator button for us. The car came, we got on, and, when it stopped at the first floor, Joe flattened against the wall, his hand on his gun. He relaxed when Joe McKenna got on.

Joe pressed 5 and, without saying a word, exited the elevator on the floor below mine. When Joe and I got off at 6, we saw Joe disappearing up the stairs to the roof. Joe went into my apartment first, even though he had left it only five minutes before to check for any new and uninvited visitors.

When Joe waved me into the house, it was just about eight o'clock. We had about two hours to wait and I was already jumpy. I made coffee for us both, only to have Joe remind me that, long before Eileen was due, there should only be one used coffee cup visible. He then regaled me for the next hour or so with stories of his FBI career.

Finally, at 9:30, Joe took his cup, washed and dried it, and put it away, saying "Ok. Let's get ready." We really had nothing to do to get ready – he disappeared into Becky's room, a room that I generally kept closed up and I paced the living room, trying to keep my emotions in check.

Finally, at about ten to ten, the doorbell rang and I went to let Eileen in. She looked exited and exciting – just gorgeous. I gave her a perfunctory kiss, while feeling her desire for more, and walked back into the living room and sat in the corner of the couch, leaning on the armrest.

She took off her jacket and, putting it and her bag next to her, sat down next to me.

"What's wrong, Jackie?"

"How's your aunt, Eileen?"

All of a sudden, she looked stricken. "You know, don't you?"

"Why don't you tell me?"

"My aunt's dead, Jackie, and she has been for a few years. She died suddenly after my mother died while you and Matty were away from the neighborhood and, since there were so few people left around here who knew us when we were a couple, I was hoping that you wouldn't have known. When you didn't express condolences as soon as we met, I just went with it. You must have seen Eddie again, right?"

I nodded "Why, Eileen?"

"I wanted to have a reason to be in the neighborhood and not just here to see you. That was why I was really here."

I stared hard at her. "Go on."

She hesitated and then went on, rapid fire. "I told you that I lived with a man that I owe a lot to. I do more than live with him; he's my husband – Bill Norris. He was Frank Ford's boss."

I stayed quiet, forcing her to go on.

"Bill knew about you being my first love. You were, Jackie, and I made such a mistake turning you away. He came to me and told me that you could link him to Frank Ford's death and that people he worked for wanted to kill you. He hoped that I could convince you to forget about any evidence that you might have. He said that it could keep him out of jail, maybe save his life, and definitely save yours."

Did he tell you to fuck me too?"

Her eyes welled up. "No, that was totally me. As soon as I saw you, I wanted you more than I did when we broke up. I think I've wanted you every day since. Bill may suspect that's what's going on but he's never said anything. We hardly talk anymore."

I stayed quiet until she went on.

"Bill was Joe's best friend. When Joe was killed in the car crash, I had two small children, a house with a big mortgage, little insurance, and I hadn't worked in five years. Bill was wonderful. He jumped in, took care of the arrangements, arranged for re-financing of the house, and hired me to do clerical work from home. I became very dependent on him and one thing led to another and we got married eighteen months after Joe's death."

She looked for a reaction from me and, when there was none, she went on.

"I never felt for Bill the way I did for Joe – or for you, Jackie – but he was wonderful to the children and was there when we needed him. When he came to me about Frank's death and you, he only asked me to speak to you. I didn't think he had anything to do with Frank's death, just that Frank might have given you information about stock market dealings that get Bill in trouble – things that he said everyone did."

"But, now, you're not so sure?"

She paused for a few seconds and then went on "No, I'm not – and that's one of the reasons that there is an estrangement. The other reason is that I realize that I never stopped loving you and I want to be with you. Bill's been more and more jumpy and pushing me about whether you've agreed to bury whatever you have. He gets calls at every hour of the day and, after every one, he gets more and more upset and pushy. I think he's coming apart."

She looked at me as though wondering whether she should say more.

"What else, Eileen?"

"I finally blew up the other night and asked him 'how could you have been involved with Frank's death? He was your and Jim's friend?' He went absolutely whacko, yelling at me – telling me that Frankie had to die because he was going to give the whole thing up – and then he said that if we didn't get this resolved soon, we could all die – him, you and me."

"Why don't you and he go to the police, Eileen, if you're afraid of being killed. We certainly know a lot of cops from the neighborhood."

"Jackie, he can't go to the police. He's guilty! If he didn't have Frankie killed directly, he knew who did it – and he probably knew before it happened – and he also did whatever he did that was wrong with the stock dealings."

"Then why don't you go, Eileen? I'll help you. I can call Joe Conway at the FBI and, I'm sure he can get you protection for yourself and your children."

"I can't do that, Jackie. I owe him too much. When all this is over – if it's ever over – I can divorce him and, if you'll still have me … but I can't help send him to prison."

"I'm sure that, if he didn't actually pull the trigger on Frankie, he could probably cut some 'state's evidence deal' to stay out of jail. He might have to go into witness protection, though."

"I can't, Jackie, and, besides, I think that he had something heavy to do with Frankie's death and I can't sent him to prison."

She stood up, grabbed her bag and coat and was reaching into the bag, probably for her car keys when Joe opened the door and stepped into the room.

"Hello, Eileen."

First, she looked confused and, then, the rage that I had seen when I told her years ago that I had been with Rita.

"Jackie, how could you set me up. I thought you loved me. I'll deny everything, anyhow. You have no proof of any of this."

"It won't do any good, Eileen, it's all on tape."

For a moment, it looked as though she would attack me and then she just collapsed into tears. Joe went to the door and opened it to let Joe and Jim in.

Joe said "You missed the excitement. We caught Serge Passarella sneaking into the house. I think he was here to kill the two of them. We grabbed him on the warrant for Frankie. If his gun matches the slugs and, based on what the Napoli thug told us, I'm sure it will, I bet he'll sing like a canary about that hit and today's adventure."

Joe looked at Eileen. "Who knew you were coming here today?"

She answered very slowly "Only Bill, But I can't believe that he'd have me killed." She looked at me. "Would he?"

"How would I know, Eileen? I don't even know him, but I believe the son-of-a-bitch would have me killed."

She fell apart, crying hysterically.

Joe looked at Joe and Jim "If Norris didn't order it, he's the next target. I better make some calls and get him arrested while he's still with us. Can you guys take her away? Hold her as a material witness. If she lawyers up, we'll charge her as an accessory to murder."

Jim nodded and they got Eileen to stand up to be cuffed and have her rights read. I just looked at them all and nodded and went into lie down.

Offering It Up

Chapter 21 -- It's A Wrap

Matty and I were having breakfast in the Capitol while I told him the whole story.

"Joe called late last night. They got the Passarella guy dead to rights, the bullets matched and he gave up Napoli; he was here to take Eileen and me out. He's a Russian who took the Passarella name to fit in with the Italian mob – but kept the name Serge. What a jerk!"

"He sounds like a lethal jerk."

"He was. He or someone else was going to kill Norris next. Joe got agents to arrest Norris before anything happened. Joe says that he is scared, scared to go to prison because he may get killed there like the Napoli thug, but scared to roll over and go into witness protection because he thinks they can find him."

"What about Eileen?"

"If he rolls, I'll think that she and her kids will go into witness protection with him. If she doesn't, they might not be safe. If he doesn't roll, I don't know what she'll do."

He put his hand over mine across the table. "And how are you, Jackie?"

"I really don't know, but I know what I have to do."

"What?"

"Offer it up."

We both laughed.

Dramatis Personae

(The following are real people who appear in "Offering It Up." None of them said or did anything attributed to them in this work of fiction. All other characters, including the protagonist Jackie Devine are fictional and exist only in my troubled mind. – John F. McMullen)

Residents of 583 West 215th Street – Mrs. Cummings, Roach, and Taylor and the Superintendent, Mr. O'Rourke.

Barbara and Jim Casey – close friends who live close to Barbara McMullen and I in nearby Putnam County; Jim is one of my oldest friends and grew up in 583 West 215th Street where much of the story is set.

Joseph Aloysius Conway – an old friend, now deceased, who, while coming from Marble Hill, a Manhattan enclave on the Bronx mainland, chose to "hang out" in Inwood. Upon graduating from Manhattan College, Joe joined the FBI.

Bob Cummings – another of my oldest friends, also from 583 West 215th Street and also now deceased.

Kevin and Matty Devine – the "real" Divines; Inwood natives – Kevin is a Paulist priest who was stationed in **Good**

Shepherd Parish twice (around his Silver Star winning service as an Army Chaplain) and now serves in Bosnia while the late Matty was an FBI agent for many years.

Jim Finn – an old friend from Inwood and a retired New York City Police Lieutenant who was a sergeant assigned to Inwood's police precinct (the 34th) at the time of the story.

Doris and Ron Friedman – friends from Yorktown, NY.

Joe Gavin — an old friend from Inwood who still lives there.

Peg and Jim Guinan – owners of the legendary *"Guinan's"* country store and bar overlooking the Hudson River in the Garrison, NY train station and the subject of **Gwendolyn Bounds'** *"little chapel by the river."* Peg had actually passed away prior to me meeting Jim but she was alive at the time of this story. Guinan's closed in 2008 when Jim moved to Florida, later dying in 2008.

Barry and Barrie Katz – friends from Jefferson Valley and the co-owners of *"The Rugged Boot"*, a shoe store housed in an old schoolhouse and a railroad caboose on Route 6 in Mohegan lake, NY.

Jim "Hobart" Lambert – an old friend who, prior to his family moving to Massachusetts, lived in the apartment in which much of the novel is set. Other friends, **Pat and Pierce Wilkerson**, now live in the same apartment.

Joe Martin and Joanne Campbell Martin- – friends from years ago who now live in the Yorktown area.

Joe McKenna and Maureen Walsh McKenna –– friends from Inwood years ago who lived in Yorktown area while Joe was an NYPD Sergeant and later a security officer. Maureen's brother, the late Jack Walsh, was a long-time friend. They have since moved from the area.

Barbara and John McMullen – my wife Barbara and I.

Claire and Jack McMullen – my real parents; Clara -- "Claire" in later years – (1901 – 1979) was a Boston native while my father John, "Jack" (1904 -1951) was a New York native and a member of the New York City Police Department when he died.

Robert McMullen – my brother, now deceased, was a college professor for 40 years, first at Iona College and then at Caldwell College. While a Christian Brother of Ireland, as principal of Power Memorial Academy, he signed Kareem

Abdul-Jabbar (then Ferdinand Lewis Alcindor)'s high school diploma.

Ed Ramos – founder and owner of "Super Business Machines."

Mike Ryan – one of my closest friends and a victim of lung cancer; I gave the toast at his wedding and the eulogy at his funeral.

Father Russell Ryan – A Paulist priest always "in love" with Good Shepherd and Inwood. He would collect birthdays from teenagers, Catholic and non-Catholic alike and for years, until his death, birthday cards indicating that he was remembering the person in his Mass would show up.

Peter Schug – a friend from the Big Apple Users' Group.

Brother Arthur Sullivan – "The Moose," legendary teacher at All Hallows High School.

Stan Veit – an old friend, my editor with *Computer Shopper Magazine*, and partner in *Web 2.0 The Magazine.*

Ed Winne – a friend since first grade, a long-time Merchant Seaman, and still a resident of Inwood.

Offering It Up

About The Author

John F. McMullen, *"johnmac the bard,"* is a poet, author, journalist, technologist, college professor, bard, denizen of cyberspace and native of the **Inwood** section of the Borough of Manhattan, city and state of New York. He is the co-author of a book on telecommunications, *"Microcomputer Communications: A Window On The World,"* the author of three collections of poetry (*"Cashing A Check," "Writing In My Head,"* and *"New and Collected Poems"* – all available on Amazon) and over 1,500 news stories, articles, & columns (*appearing in such publications as Computer Shopper, The Chicago Tribune, InfoWorld, Lear's, PC Magazine, National Review, and Newsbytes*), and academic papers. Additionally, he is the editor of *"Web 2.0 The Magazine"* (*web2themag.com*) and the administrator of a number of Internet Mailing Lists and Social Networks (*including two focused on Inwood*). He resides in Jefferson Valley, NY with his wife **Barbara E. McMullen**, an educator and entrepreneur. He is the father of **Claire Cleary McMullen**, a New York City businesswoman, and **Luke J. McMullen**, a Hollywood screenwriter. He may be reached at *johnmac13@gmail.com*.

He is currently working on the second novel in the *"Inwood Tale"* series, *"Rita"*, while continuing to write poetry and short stories.

Made in the USA
Columbia, SC
29 May 2025